Three Questions

OTHER WRITINGS BY EUGENE A. KELLY

FOR WHAT IT'S WORTH:
A Guide for New Stockbrokers (1985)

FOR WHAT IT'S WORTH:
A Guide for New Financial Advisors (2001)

THE PENDULUM LETTER (1990–2019)

UNDER THE NAME E. ALY

107 SECRETS TO SUCCESS
FOR THE GRADUATE (2019)

FOR WHAT IT'S WORTH essays (2019–)

CHANGE HAPPENS But Will They Understand? (2021)

FORTHCOMING

FOR WHAT IT'S WORTH:
19 Rules for Getting Rich and Staying That Way
Despite Wall Street (January 2022)

Three Questions

Stories

E. Aly

Marshwinds Press Company

ISBN 978-0-9614496-9-8 (Hardback)
978-1-7341170-0-4 (Paperback)
978-1-7341170-1-1 (epub)

Library of Congress Control Number: 2021920055

Subjects: FICTION/ Short Stories

Book Club virtual readings and Q&A sessions are available by contacting:
Marshwinds Press Company
P. O. Box 21099
St. Simons Island, GA 31522
1-800-343-3751

OR go to **uniquereads.com**

Printed in the United States of America

Cover & Interior Design: Creative Publishing Book Design

For Judy,
who makes it all possible.

Contents

Beach Walk

THE INCOMING TIDE WASHING Anita's feet could not wash away her unhappiness. Just as steadily as the ocean tides, the tears flowed down her cheeks in rivulets, dropping on the white linen shirt almost covering her red cotton shorts. She let the tears flow. Her mother had taught her that tears were unhappiness leaving the body. She guessed she'll be crying for days. Looking to her left at the ocean, Anita wondered if it resulted from Mother Nature's tears of unhappiness at how humans treat the planet.

God, how she wished she could have another confrontation with her mother! This time Anita would pay greater attention to the repetitive drilling of ideas into her mind. She reached into her right shorts pocket and pulled out a travel pack of tissues. Extracting one, she blew her nose and then stuck it in her left shorts pocket, now bulging with wet tissues.

The one piece of motherly advice looping in Anita's mind was the one about marriage: "Marriage is like a garden: you must tend it every day or weeds and vines will choke it."

Anita had always shouted back, "It takes two to tango!" That seemed more appropriate to her. Too bad most men didn't know how to garden or tango. All they seemed to do was play golf. Yeah, it took two to tango. A mental picture of a muscular man in a tight, striped T-shirt materialized, with biceps and chest muscles stretching the fabric and a flat waist without stomach flab or love handles. He wore a pair of black stovepipe pants ending just above shiny black boots. She could not make out his face. He was dominating a beautiful woman with long, dark hair; deep red lipstick; and breasts struggling to be free from the scoop-necked dress that ended in flowing fabric two inches above her black four-inch-heeled pumps. She could see the woman was herself. She would love to learn to tango. Why couldn't she see who the man was? His body looked like Dave's body when they had gotten married twenty years before. Now, if he put on that outfit, the shirt would make Dave look like an upside down hundred-watt light bulb. Well, perhaps not a hundred-watt bulb, but for sure a sixty-watt bulb. She sobbed, and the tears flowed more. Why were mothers always right? How had her garden become so overgrown with weeds and vines? An anguished moan involuntarily escaped from deep inside her.

The surf sent sand between her toes. How she loved the feeling of the ocean, the sand, and the breeze! She openly sobbed, not caring if anyone saw her. Dawn was breaking. The sky was overcast, but the clouds were thin and weren't rain clouds. The easterly breeze was pushing them westward. She turned and faced the east, waiting for the burst of fire at the horizon. She could feel the tides scouring the sand around her feet until she slowly sank down. The sun's brightness illuminated the sky with orange and pink behind the clouds, and a single fireball rose, fulfilling its daily duty of promising a new beginning for all who took notice. A new day to achieve the happiness they wanted. Anita started sobbing again. Twenty years before, she and Dave had spent their honeymoon at this same beach, in the same rental cottage they had reserved each year since. She and Dave had stood holding hands and promising their life would always have them loving each other as much as they did those two weeks. They had promised to watch the sunrise together whenever they were here. Now, she stood here alone. What had happened?

In the early years, what they called the BC era, their code for "before children," they would come down before dawn with a beach towel, make love in a swale in the sand dunes, and look at the stars. They had both professed their love for each other, confident of God's blessing if they were fortunate to see a shooting star. As the sun rose, they had stood in the surf and promised anew to love each other as they did at that moment. What had changed? Who had stopped this love ritual? She did. He did. They both did. You can't have sex in the sand dunes before dawn with babies and toddlers alone in the rental house. Other times, crying children and sleep deprivation dissipated the sunrise magic. She and Dave's love renewal ritual had slipped away just like the tide went out. But at least the tide came back in twice a day, every day. Scanning the expanse of ocean, she wondered: can our love come back in?

She continued to follow the contour of the surf's edge as the tide inched higher and higher toward the sand dunes. Her bare feet tickled, accompanying the crushing noise as the shells at the water's edge gave way to her weight. It was a fitting metaphor for the way life had crushed the dreams they'd had twenty years before. It seemed like only yesterday they married in their junior year of college and the world had been theirs for the taking. The decades of their twenties and thirties, and now their fortieth year, evaporated. Gone where? She kicked at the foam created by the tide. Dave was going to conquer the business world, and they were going to have two children, a boy and a girl—at least they had gotten that right. She was going to have a "mad money" career with the freedom to be the mom she wanted to be. They were going to retire at fifty, travel to beaches around the world, drink wine, and discover the interesting and unique to enrich their lives. Dreams. Reality reared its ugly head when they both realized she needed to have a real paying job once the kids entered school. His salary was not enough to cover the essentials and have the extras like their friends had. He enjoyed his job but not enough to give up his golf time to get ahead. Anita's tears almost dried up with anger. The anger faded quickly, but it had been there. Was she angry with Dave? Herself? Her mother? Everyone? She kicked the foam every few steps, wondering if she could admit her anger was really disappointment that her once knight in shining armor turned out to be a serf instead. Would she have married him twenty years ago if he had said to her, "I really don't want to conquer the world. I just want a cushy job, making enough to get by as long as you get a job too." Would she have? She looked up at the clouds with patches of blue between them. Yes, she admitted silently. She loved the man, not his ambition, which was an extra. She still loved the man, even in his current sixty-watt-bulb state.

Anita realized her whole social circle was going through the midlife-crisis phase of life. Carol and Henry had separated the previous year and were in a divorce struggle worthy of the movies. Their children suffered and felt confused. Emily and Dave Jr. had them for sleepovers often. Anita had tried to help the children understand their parents loved them but that sometimes marriages didn't work out.

Maria and Carl had moved from the neighborhood into a community with a guarded gate, community center, pool, golf course, and tennis courts. Even though they left less than six months ago, the communications had become fewer and fewer. Maria had called two weeks before to say their children would go to private school in the fall rather than public school, so she had resigned as the PTA president and class representative. Did Anita want her to propose she take over?

"No, thank you; I'm too busy at work," Anita had said.

Barbara and Steve bought a beach house around the corner from the one she and Dave had rented all those years. Barbara and Steve liked to slip away to their new love nest when their children were at sleepovers. According to Barbara, it had rekindled their passions. His company had picked Steve for the senior management track, while Barbara had won the tennis championship for women aged forty and over at the club.

Out of the corner of her eye, she saw part of a shell. She stopped walking. She nudged it with her toes. It gave way easily, and the surf washed it. She bent down and picked it up. It was unbroken. Her delight was complete. All these years the *Cyphoma gibbosum* shell, better known to avid shellers as the Flamingo Tongue, had eluded her. She tumbled it over and over to see if it was complete. This one was perfect and special because it had the mantle of the animal extended on the shell. Her collection had only unbroken shells; that was what made them special and still interesting to collect. Anita felt that whenever something or someone had a high standard, the results were more interesting. That included a seashell collection—and marriage. The summer she was pregnant with Emily, she had bought the best shell book she could find and memorized the names and pictures of all the shells on the beach. That was the year she had made the rule: a shell had to be unbroken for admittance into her unique shell collection. She sighed. One good thing happened every time she walked the beach. Her tears dried up. She went to put the shell in her shorts pocket and realized she might need to go back in for tissues, so she carefully put it in her shirt pocket. Even if she was the only one in the family who appreciated the collection, that was okay. She knew the dreams and thrills she experienced while finding the shells. Neither child really cared for the beach. Even when they were young, Emily had resisted leaving the air-conditioned house because she didn't want to get sandy. Dave Jr. had been afraid of monsters underneath the ocean coming up and getting them. He hadn't even seen the movie *Jaws*. She noticed he and his buddies were more interested in coming to the beach now, since the girls they knew would wear bikinis.

Anita blew her nose. Positive thoughts. No more negative ones. I'm on hallowed ground, she reminded herself, just me and Mother Nature. Just positive thoughts. No more tears.

She and Dave were there alone. The home equity line of credit had paid for the children to go to summer camp in the mountains. They had two weeks alone, the first in fourteen years. When they had arrived the previous night, they pleaded tiredness. Dave had drunk his customary six beers before and during dinner, and she'd had her three glasses of Cab. She had thought they might walk on the beach, go back to the house, shower, and have sex, but that fantasy disappeared by the time she finished the dishes, and he was snoring in his chair.

Thinking of the children caused her eyes to burn. No, she will not cry. Only happy thoughts. How can you have happy thoughts when your fourteen-year-old daughter says you are stupid and overbearing, one of the few times she said over one word, while rolling her eyes?

While packing Emily's clothes for summer camp, Anita had picked up her phone and seen text after text from a boy named Frank.

"Who is Frank?" she had asked Emily.

"None of your business," Emily had replied, snatching the phone from Anita's hands.

If that wasn't bad enough, Dave had received a call at work from the country club golf pro. Dave Jr. and some friends, horsing around, had let a cart go into the lake on the eighth hole. Someone would have to pay for the ruined cart, and the boys could not play the course until September. When he confronted his son, who denied any of it, Junior called his father crazy. What had happened to the two perfect children being raised by perfect parents?

"Just positive thoughts," she sensed Mother Nature saying.

"Positive thoughts," Anita repeated.

The tide continued nudging her up the beach toward the sand dunes. The dunes—special places with special pre-dawn memories. Positive thoughts. She'd take the first step in rekindling the beach romance of the past. She may not be as thin and curvy as in the past, but she must still be attractive. William sure thought so. William, he wanted some. Every day at work, he found a reason to speak to her, to compliment her on something she had done or worn or said. He wasn't hard on the eyes; that was for sure. If David was a sixty-watt lightbulb, William was six years younger and as thin as a florescent light tube. She giggled at the thought of a florescent light glowing from his crotch. He had all but come out and asked her to have an affair. She almost said yes, but could not do it. She still loved Dave as much as ever. If only he found her as attractive as he used to and as William did now. She smiled, remembering what had driven Dave crazy with desire so many years before.

She picked up the pace of her stroll. She wanted to make the end of the Spit before the tide completely covered the beach. There were too many sand spurs for walking barefoot in the wild dunes and forest of the Spit. When she could see the groin separating the developed beach from the wild Spit, she angled away from the water and toward the sand path over the groin. As she cut through the dunes, she looked for a spot where the swale hid anyone from prying eyes. She thought about the only thing she would wear the next morning: the short pale blue sundress with the strapless elasticized top. She knew just what beach towel she'd bring. Positive thoughts. Yes, Mother Nature, positive thoughts.

Crossing the groin, Anita saw the shorebirds several hundred yards ahead at the water's edge. At this distance she couldn't quite make out all the species, but she was sure there were piping plovers, maybe a Wilson plover or two, sandpipers, and terns. She did not see any black skimmers at work but was confident they would appear soon. She almost hated to walk toward them. Shorebirds are skittish when people invade their domain. The guard birds, of which there are always some of each species, would signal the gathering of fifty to a hundred birds that a human or a predator was close. The birds would take flight, circle as one, and re-land either back behind the threat or farther up the beach. She was absent for a year, so they didn't know it was her. Or did they? Every year on the last day of her beach time, she could approach the birds, whispering to them, and they would not bolt as she strolled through the mass of birds and continued down the beach.

Can one love wild creatures like birds? She thought so. Can those same creatures know a person loves them and return that love in their own way? Can two miles of beach change the course of life? Anita looked at the ocean just as a porpoise broke the surface. The chill she always felt when seeing this majestic scene coursed through her. It was then she realized she was in the middle of the shorebirds. They didn't fly. She was where she should be. Dave could be where he needed to be. These two weeks at the beach would fill their pleasant memory bank, again.

Young Love

ELIZABETH CAMBRIDGE WAS TROUBLED. The growing season of 1834 had been a good one. She looked over her potato fields, the five workers forking them up, and the horse and cart being loaded with potato sacks for banking in her yard. The number of potatoes harvested should have translated into more money than she had in her strong box. Someone was stealing from her. Who? It couldn't be the sweet Isabella or her half-brother John. No, they were loyal and lived in the house with her. Perhaps it was Shepard, she thought. A month ago, suspecting Shepard and Isabella were becoming too close, she told Shepard he could not sleep in the house any longer.

"She confronted me before she left for London," Isabella cried as Shepard's hands roamed her body under her night-clothes. "You promised she would never know. You promised I wouldn't get caught. What are we to do?"

"Did she find all of the money you have stolen?"

"Nay, she only knew about what I had in my purse."

"Well, my love, I have a plan. When is she due back from London?"

"This afternoon, before tea."

"Good, give me the rest of the money. I'll keep it so she can't find it when she returns." He kissed her neck and pulled her to him. "If we can get rid of her, we could sell her potatoes in London."

"Get rid of her? How?"

"As I look around this property, I see cribs of corn, sacks of potatoes, chickens, horses, and two cows. She must control the rats, or else they would be overrunning the property."

"Aye, she has that nitwit Thomas spread arsenic around, mixed with sugar and oatmeal."

"Ah, my love, you are brilliant! Do you know where the arsenic is stored?"

"Up there," she pointed to the rafters in the washroom, where they were now lying on the clean laundry.

"You said she will be back before tea, right? Do you think she will take tea this afternoon?"

"Always, it is a ritual. My brother and I must join her every day. She prattles on about how lazy the workers are or the low potato prices at market."

"Oh, my most beautiful flower, perhaps you could mix some arsenic in with the tea, and then our problems would be solved. Before anyone would know she was dead, we could sell the potatoes at market and be on our way to Scotland."

"Tell me, my strong one, what to do." Isabella maneuvered herself into position.

"Give me the money for safekeeping in case she returns early. After I'm gone, mix some of the arsenic in with the tea. I will meet you at the road where it crosses the river at noon. We will stay away tonight. Before dawn, I'll come back and hitch the horse and load the cart with sacks of potatoes and meet you on the road in Tottenham. If we are stopped, we'll say the trip to market was planned by the Missus."

"Oh, yes, yes, it is a good plan." Isabella was lost in the ecstasy of her love, not thinking of the consequences for her brother nor of the fact Shepard may not be waiting for her when she came to meet him at noon later that day nor the feel of the gallows rope.

She Was His Memory That Would Not Fade

HAROLD FELT HAPPY. HE liked his life even though it wasn't what he'd dreamed about as a boy or even as a young adult, full of vim and vigor, ready to conquer the world. As most people find out when they begin life's journey, the effort takes a great deal of attitude, courage, hard work, and luck, not to mention the right choices. Life itself builds friction, slowing down the drive most people have in their twenties. There are only twenty-four hours in a day, and society determines how most of those hours will unfold. Successful aspirants spend seven hours a day sleeping, eight to nine hours working, and the remaining nine with family, friends, church, and community activities. That's why when they reach midlife, many achievers have a crisis of identity and question why they're living the lives they are. Some of

Harold's friends jettisoned their pleasant lives and tried to reinvent themselves, seeking to recover the fire in the belly that would make them masters of their destiny. Not Harold. When the restlessness stirred, making him think of what could have been or should have been, he already knew he had made that decision in his youth. He soldiered on and ascended another rung on the ladder of social acceptance and success, while some of his comrades were falling off the ladder altogether. Being the executive vice president of a local business was the goal set for him, and he'd achieved it.

Mack's was his favorite coffee shop in a historic neighborhood bristling with new-age and exotic cafés. It was strategically in the heart of this fashionable and exciting section of town. Open from 7:00 a.m. until 2:00 p.m. seven days a week, it hosted students with blue hair and multiple tattoos mixing congenially with professors and working people. Mack's was the mecca, the epicenter, the heart of the daytime social scene. It was on the southeast corner of Wharf Street, a north-south artery in the city, and Lee Street, a two-way street running east and west, shaded by decades-old oak trees and townhouses, some built over a century ago. It had been closed for a week of deep cleaning and renovation. Today was the reopening.

When Harold walked through the newly painted door, the transformation overwhelmed him. The floor was the same black-and-white tiles. Tables were the same wrought-iron legs with marble tops. Cushioned wooden chairs were familiar, but with clean fabric coverings. The counter and refrigerated case were the same, filled with deli meats, cheeses, and desserts.

What was different were the walls. Instead of a dingy, aged cream color, the walls were a stark, bright white. Hanging on them in gold frames were oil paintings, each with its own spotlight. Some were representational landscapes and portraits. Others were abstract paintings of such depth and meaning that the art almost shouted at the viewer. Some were impressionistic paintings, evoking visceral emotions of love and happiness. The exhibit showed such a wide range of skill and talent that it overcame Harold with awe. He was most interested in learning about these artists. Where did they live? Were they local? Did they have a studio where he could see more? Where did they learn their skills? He put his briefcase on what he considered "his" table and draped his jacket over the back of the chair. Going to the counter, he placed his order with the young lady, who most likely was a student at the college. It was then that he noticed the framed sign, which read:

My family has collected the art on the walls over the last forty years. In the summer of 1980, my dad hired a young lady, Emily Aliffi, to work in the restaurant. Emily would become an accomplished artist. While she only worked here a short time, my dad knew she was talented and committed to her dream. When she announced it was time to go to New York, he purchased two sketchbooks of drawings she had made in town. This money gave her

Pride and jealousy gripped Harold. He looked around at the paintings again. All were hers! Emily had done what she said she would do. He could have done what she did. He helped with her accomplishments. Looking again at the announcement, he relished seeing her. Mack had bought the two sketchbooks Harold had given her. He smiled again. Taking his coffee and scone, he sat so he could examine each piece, one by one, moving his chair around the table. He would definitely be here tomorrow at four! It would be so good to see her again. They would have plenty to talk about, for sure.

* * *

Mack's was the first coffee shop he found when he moved to town as a bachelor engaged to a socialite's daughter. As a recent college graduate, Harold experienced a golden period of carefreeness between graduation and his wedding in August, when his climb up the ladder of success would begin. He had three months to nurse his genuine passion: art. Every morning he left his room at the boarding house, carrying his artist's satchel and wearing blue jeans, a T-shirt, and boat shoes without socks. He went to Mack's, enjoying coffee and a cranberry orange scone while examining and studying his sketchbook's pencil drawings from the prior day. The historic district fascinated him with its evenly spaced parks emblazoned with their monuments to heroic citizens of the past, its old houses in various stages of aging, its government buildings showing the egos of past city leaders, and, most of all, the bluff and river marking the northern end of the city. He studiously applied the personal guidance his artist grandfather taught him during his childhood, polished by his two elective art classes in college. Harold was the happiest when he was in the bubble of artistry. As he explored the city looking for suitable scenes to memorialize in his sketchbook, his eye was like a wide lens, seeing everything in detail, absorbing so much in perspective until the right vision appeared. Once it did, his hand flew across the paper and his concentration made him oblivious to everything outside the focal point he captured in his mind's eye. The following day, over coffee and a scone, he critiqued his previous day's work, rating each drawing as to its technical and aesthetic quality. He had used this grading method for years. Now, most drawings were B+ or better. By noon he was off again, searching for his discovery of the day.

Two weeks after he started his routine, he was sitting with his coffee and scone, engrossed in his sketchbook, when he heard, "More coffee?" Looking up, he saw an interesting girl—not beautiful or cute, just intriguing. The impression was lasting. The oversized green blouse she wore enhanced her emerald-green eyes. Fiery red hair, hanging in silky smooth curls, rested gently on her shoulders. Even smiling, her mouth was small, but it competed with her eyes for attention. Her face was pale and bore no makeup to hide its character. Her worn-but-not-torn jeans were too big, held up by a sweat-stained, cracked, brown leather belt, obviously older than her. Instead of the flip-flops most youths wore that summer, Emily wore scuffed hiking boots with string laces. What was it about her that riveted his attention? Harold didn't know. He only knew he wanted to be her friend, not romantically, but a friend who said hello, asked how she was, and chit-chatted about what was happening in the city.

"Yes, please," he said, pushing his coffee cup to the other side of the table.

"What are you studying?" she asked, pouring the coffee.

"Oh, some doodling and drawings I do for fun."

"I want to see," she said, putting the coffeepot on the table and spinning the sketchbook around before Harold could protest. She studied the drawing, turned the page, and studied the next. Continuing to flip the pages and looking intently at each page, sometimes running her finger along the lines of the sketches, she said nothing.

"Emily, order up!" came booming from the kitchen. Picking up the coffeepot, she whirled around and disappeared. Harold sat there, embarrassed. She didn't like his work. A stranger, not a relative or friend who felt obliged to say the work was good, didn't like his efforts. She was polite enough not to be negative, but he could tell—she hadn't said a word, which said everything. He put his sketchbook in his satchel, shoved the rest of the scone in his mouth, took a sip of coffee, and stood. He couldn't get out of Mack's fast enough.

Walking north through the parks along Wharf Street, he headed to the place he felt safe as an artist. Passing the cathedral with tourists finishing their morning tour, he thought about stopping at the church or diverting to the old cemetery one block over, but he didn't. The sting of rejection was too new. His safe place, under the great canopy of the live oak tree on the river bluff, was where he could recover his confidence. The eternal movement of the water coming from the plains and mountains to the west and meeting the Atlantic Ocean twenty miles to the east would ease his anxiety. The riverfront was an endless opportunity to capture both nature and humans in the cycle of a day's activity. He could sit there all day, hungrily taking inspiration from the small activities of life. Drawing with deliberate discipline restored confidence in his abilities. Who was she to dismiss his work so callously? Going back to Mack's, facing that girl who so quickly dismissed his work, would be too much. His work was good, perhaps very good, but obviously not good enough for her. Who was she, anyway?

What credentials did she have to judge his work? His hand continued to fill the bright white, heavy stock pages.

Harold stayed away from Mack's the next day. But habits, particularly pleasant ones, are hard to break, so he was at his table the day after that. He studied his drawings intently, keeping his head down to avoid seeing her. Suddenly, a notebook page landed on his sketchbook. When he looked up, she was standing there, hands on her hips, green eyes sparkling like two emeralds in a spotlight. He looked back down at the paper. Ignoring the ruled lines, the material on the back of the paper, and the jagged edge where she ripped it from a spiral binder, he saw a remarkable pencil drawing of a house. He even recognized the house, the details perfectly capturing the personality of the structure.

"Did you do this?" he asked, looking back up at her.

"Yes. I looked for you yesterday but missed you. I wanted to show you some of my work. You're so much better than I am. I just wanted to get your opinion about where I need to improve."

Harold's chest seized up as he hyperventilated. Not only did she like his work, but she was an artist! She was someone who understood the effort put into a drawing!

"Yes, well, you have talent. A lot of talent. This is not the place for the conversation we need to have. What time do you get off work?"

"Two. I can meet you anywhere it's convenient for you if you have time and interest."

"I have both. Why don't you meet me at the river bluff? Walk straight up Wharf until you come to the river. There's a stately old oak tree with a bench beneath its canopy. I'll be there. One question, please: why do you use writing notebook paper for your drawings?"

"I get the notebooks out of the trash at the college. I can't afford sketchbooks like you have. Besides, I throw away the ones that I feel didn't turn out right."

"You should never throw away your disappointments. Those are what you learn from. We can talk about that and much more later. By the way, I'm Harold Everett," he said.

"I'm Emily. Emily Aliffi. I look forward to talking with you this afternoon, Harry." She smiled, crinkled her nose, turned, and left. Harold left her drawing in his sketchbook and closed it.

* * *

Waiting for Emily, Harold tried to draw, but his hand shook, and he couldn't even manage a straight line. Why was he so nervous? He didn't have any romantic feelings for her. My God, he had just met the girl and was already engaged to the love of his life. What he felt was an exhilaration that she'd recognized the quality of his artistry. She was a kindred spirit who loved art as much as he did, someone he could talk art with. He spent the last hour going over her drawing. She was quite gifted, just inexperienced. Her talent was shining through like a lighthouse beacon in a fog. Here I am, it shouted! Here's your dream port! Come through the fog of my inexperience and find the true talent! He wouldn't point out her flaws or shortcomings. He would ask her questions, lead her toward the realization of what worked and what didn't.

She arrived shortly after two with more pages in an envelope.

"Harry, I really appreciate your looking at my work. I don't know your story, but you are really, really good. Anything you see that needs improvement, please, please tell me."

"Certainly, I will. But I'm going to ask you to do the same for me. I may be further down the art path than you, but I need a critical, unbiased eye looking at my work as well. Let's set one ground rule: all criticism will be in the spirit of helping each other get better—guidance taken from one professional speaking to another. Agreed?"

"Agreed."

"Since you're calling me Harry, may I call you Em?"

"Yeah, that's cool. Em. I like it, Harry."

"One last thing before we begin." Harry reached into his satchel, which was sitting between them, and pulled out two eight-by-eleven-inch hardback sketchbooks. "These are for you: a gift designed to make my job easier. In the next several weeks, you will hopefully fill them with your work."

"Harry, I don't know what to say. Thank you. I've never had a real sketchbook before. Thank you!" She ran her hand over the black covers, opening one and fanning the pages. The look she gave Harry said more than words could have.

For the next eight weeks, Em and Harry met during the week from two-fifteen until five-thirty. They examined one of her drawings and one of his on the same subject. In the beginning, the differences between the two drawings were significant. Toward the end of the time, there were differences but not in skill, just style.

It was the Monday of the last week before Harry's wedding when Em asked him, "Harry, have you ever thought about a life as an artist?"

"No. That's not in the cards for me. This coming weekend, as you know because you're invited, I'm getting married. When I return from my honeymoon, I'll start work at Houlihan's Ship Chandlery."

"Haven't you ever dreamed of being an artist full time?"

"Oh, yes, I've dreamed. Dreams are for dreamers. I'm a realist. My soon-to-be wife expects, as she should, a husband who will achieve for her and their future children, make the family's place in society, and be an active member of the community. Do you dream of being an artist?"

"No, I no longer dream of being an artist. I *am* an artist. A life of creativity, willing to do what it takes to succeed, is what I will have. I know you love your wife, but have you ever asked her if she would give you moral support as you build yourself a life as an artist? If she loves you as much as you love her, she will support your efforts in the early years."

Harold looked at the river and the sun dappling off the swirling current. Would Julie go for his being an artist? He really didn't know.

"I don't know. I'll ask her this evening while we're at dinner."

"I bet she'll say yes," Em said, turning animated. "Harry, you have the natural talent and empathy to be a great artist. Just think, we could get one of these old warehouses for a studio. Both of us work part-time jobs and meet every day to draw and paint. Exhibitions in our studio to sell our work could sustain us until we found a gallery that would represent us. We could inspire each other! We can do this. Please ask Julie. Please!"

"We could conquer the art world!" Harry shouted, catching her excitement. "I'll bring up the subject this evening. Now, we only have this week before I'm gone for two weeks, so let's have some fun drawing."

* * *

Julie and Harold were in her parents' drawing room. She sat on his lap, kissing him passionately, his hands caressing her breasts through her dress.

"Oh, God, I want you," she whispered, kissing his eyes and biting his ear. "Less than a week—I'll probably strip you naked in the church and jump on you as soon as the bishop says we're man and wife." She giggled at the thought.

"On the altar, my dear. I'll hike up your wedding dress and enter you right there on the altar. Everyone will know we're married. They won't blame me because you are so beautiful."

They heard a noise on the stairs and Julie jumped up, went to the other side of the room, and sat in a chair.

"Where is dinner, Harold?" she asked, flipping the pages of a magazine.

"I thought we would walk to that new steakhouse on Main Street. I don't know the name, but I've heard it's good."

"Wonderful choice."

As they strolled through the parks and tree-lined streets, Harold said, "Julie, you know I'm passionate about my art. What if I wanted to be a full-time artist? There are some who feel I have a God-given talent and could be a success. It could take a while to get established, but when I became successful, the rewards would be huge. What do you think?"

Julie took his hand in hers and said, "Harold, don't be silly. I know you love your art, but it's just a hobby. You wouldn't be happy as a starving artist, watching me and our children possibly hungry and destitute. Besides, how would we fit into our social circle if you aren't in a management role at some well-established company in town? Silly, think of the favor Daddy did in getting that nice Mr. Houlihan to give you an opportunity. You know he doesn't have any children who are interested in taking over his business. All you must do is work hard and be around when he wants to retire. You can pretend you're an artist on the weekends whenever the children and I don't want you to pay attention to us. God, I can't wait to make babies, my handsome Harold hunk." She squeezed his hand as they entered the restaurant.

* * *

It wasn't until Thursday that Em again brought up joining forces as fully committed artists. "You have mentioned nothing about becoming a full-time artist. Have you thought about it? Did you talk to Julie?"

"It's all I've thought about since Monday, and yes, I talked to Julie. She's opposed. Her father has arranged for me to have a position in a terrific business where the owner wants to retire in twenty years and doesn't have any children willing to take over. I can't disappoint her. I doubt she would even marry me if I announced I was going to be a full-time artist. Em, if we had met a year ago, I'd commit one hundred percent to having a studio with you and the two of us becoming accomplished artists. I want that terribly, but it's not in the cards at this point." Harry looked at her. Her eyes had lost their sparkle. Maybe it was the light, or maybe it was the words. Her chin quivered slightly. She visibly took a deep breath and tried to smile.

"Harry, you have as deep a talent for art as I've ever encountered. It's a tragedy you won't exploit it. The world will miss the beauty of your mind, but you'll suffer more because you won't achieve what God wanted you to. These past few weeks have been the happiest time of my life. I've learned so much. I no longer have doubts about myself and my art. Thank you for that." Em placed her sketchbook in her oversized purse, stood, and looked down at Harry. She leaned over and kissed him on the forehead then turned and walked away.

He did not go to Mack's that Friday, the day before his wedding. It was after he returned from his honeymoon that he showed up for his coffee and scone. Instead of his satchel, he carried a briefcase. He wore a suit and tie as a member of good standing in the business community. When he inquired about Emily while ordering his coffee and cranberry orange scone, the young lady at the counter said Emily had left town a week ago. Headed for New York City, she'd told everyone. She was going to be a successful artist.

* * *

At three o'clock Harold, carrying his satchel, claimed his table. She would remember the satchel. The leather was dry and brittle, its threading fraying after years in the attic. He couldn't get all the dust from around the buckles. Still, it was a genuine artist's satchel, able to carry everything an artist needed, even sketchbooks or a small canvas. Not finding any of his sketchbooks, he asked Julie where they might be, and she told him she had thrown them out when they'd moved into her family home six years ago.

The café was filling up. The chatter between patrons was reverberating off the tile floor, echoing along with the oohs and ahs from the crowd, snaking around the room, moving from picture to picture. Harold joined the procession, studying the brushstrokes and the powerful use of color. He understood the ramifications of the choice he'd made. At the second painting, he recognized a little style quirk he had noticed in her drawings so many years ago. He doubled back, and there it was in the first painting, too. His friends Bill and Mary Sue Cunningham were standing next to him.

Bill looked away from the painting and said, "Harold, good to see you. Is Julie here?"

"No, she's at a church meeting. Beautiful work, eh?"

"Outstanding."

"You know, she and I drew together when she was here forty years ago. We'd go to the river bluff and all the parks, sketching and discussing art. She was just learning, and I had taken art in college."

"You don't say. She really has talent."

Harold followed the flow of people. How could he raise the question about her style quirk so she would know how much he thought of their time together? Just noticing it would tell her how interested he was in her work. No one else would even see it. He was pleased and excited at the thought of their pending reunion. In the fourth picture, he noticed confusion in her brushstrokes. She was hesitant in what she was doing. He'd ask, professionally, the question that pointed out the change in confidence, like he did forty years ago—two peers helping each other.

"Harold, what do you think? I believe if I could play golf as well as this Aliffi woman paints, I could be the next Tiger Woods," the man standing beside him said.

"Oh, hello, Steven. Yes, she's good."

"Not good—great! I wonder what her paintings sell for."

"No idea, but I'm sure it's a lot," Harold said. It was at this moment that his carefully constructed defense mechanism failed.

Choking briefly on his breath, he realized how successful he could have been if he had made the right choice. Back then, he was better than she was. Working together, he could have reached or exceeded her level of expertise. He could have been the artist she saw in him. Pain shot through his stomach like a hot poker. He went back to his table and collapsed in his seat. He moved the satchel from the tabletop onto the chair next to him. It was no longer a source of pride, but a badge of cowardice. He could have, should have, would have, and that's all there was to it. A greater chance most people never get. He'd made the wrong choice.

At four, he heard young Mack call for attention. Harold looked up and saw Em. He would have recognized her in any crowd. Her hair was still reddish, with streaks of gray. It still draped on her shoulders in silky curls, as it had when she was a young woman. She still wore no makeup; the age lines around her eyes and mouth were more like frames around beautiful paintings. Her emerald eyes still held the same fiery glow, taking in all of her surroundings. Expensive tailored clothes instead of thrift shop secondhand garments fit her still youthful, trim body.

Mack held onto Emily's elbow, ushering her from one person to another, introducing her to the crowd. They came closer. Harold stood and waited for his turn. He would suggest they get together and catch up on their art after the reception or the next morning. She finally stood before him. He smiled, and she smiled.

He heard Mack say, "Harold, this is Emily Aliffi. Emily, this is Harold Everett."

"How do you do, Mr. Everett? So nice of you to come," Emily said. Then she and Mack moved on. Harold stood speechless. Should he turn and call her nickname, Em? Should he shout out, "Emily, it's me, Harry! Remember, you wanted us to get a studio together forty years ago?" She was his memory that would not fade away. He was not even a distant memory from her youth. Harold picked up his satchel and walked out the door.

Three Questions

"M S. ELWOOD, THIS IS Ms. Christian, again. You need to come pick Stephen up, again."

"Ms. Christian, I'm at work. I can't leave. Just put him in the library or somewhere until school is over. There's nothing I can do." The phone line went dead.

Ms. Christian listened to the dial tone. It was only second period, but the crisis had escalated. She looked at Stephen, who was sitting on the other side of her desk. His facial features looked defiant. His eyes looked afraid. He seemed to sense that his mother had hung up. The seventh grade is a tough time for a young boy, and they had held Stephen back in the first grade, so he was one walking, talking rage of hormones. Too many hormones to act like a child, but too few to act like a man. He'd been acting up in classes since September, particularly during his second-period science class. She'd seen it before. Young men got to this point in their lives, and the lack of discipline and guidance from an absent father showed. What to do? Well, that was what they paid her the big bucks to figure out. She smiled, thinking about the big bucks. She could barely keep her family moving forward. Stephen thought she was smiling at him and planning to let him off with lunch detention. He smiled back.

"Okay, Stephen. For the rest of the day, you're going to sit in the reception area with my secretary. Do you have any homework that has to be turned in for your other classes?"

"I don't know," Stephen answered with a smirk.

"Gee, that's a shame. No problem. Come with me." Ms. Christian rose from her chair and walked around the desk. Stephen didn't move. She went over to her office door and closed it. Walking back toward Stephen, she came up behind him and swung her arm, catching the back of his head with her palm. Stephen went sprawling out of his chair, his backpack flying off his lap. Catching himself on the edge of her desk, he looked back at her, wide-eyed.

"You can't do that!" he shouted. "I'm going to tell my mother and the cops!" He sat back down in the chair, rubbing the back of his head, his eyes burning.

Trying not to show how badly her hand hurt, Ms. Christian grabbed a handful of his shirt, leaned down, and put her lips inches from his ear. "You tell anybody you want. I'll deny it, and you can't prove it. Next time I tell you to do something, you'd better do it without hesitation. Now, follow me."

Stephen picked up his backpack and followed her into the outer office.

"Ms. Coty, Mr. Elwood is going to sit at that desk over in the corner. He is not to get up, speak, or leave for any reason, even to go to the bathroom, before the last bell rings. Got it?"

Ms. Coty looked at Stephen and back at Ms. Christian. "Yes, ma'am."

"Good. Please give me a new yellow tablet and eight sharpened pencils."

Ms. Coty opened her right-side desk drawer and removed a new yellow pad. She took a fistful of pencils from the center drawer and counted out eight, then handed it all to Ms. Christian.

"Stephen, there are fifty pages in this tablet. I want you to number the pages, one to fifty, in the top right corner without tearing the pages off the tablet. You understand?"

"Yes, ma'am."

"Now, write on the first line, neatly so it fits on the line: only I am responsible for my actions. Go on, write it. I want to make sure you get all of it on one line."

Stephen did as he was told.

"Stephen, there are thirty-nine lines to a page. There are fifty pages. You're going to write that sentence on every line of every page between now and the time I leave at four-thirty. There will be no lunch break. You are going to sit at that desk until you're finished. If you finish before four-thirty, you must bring the tablet to me for inspection. Understand?"

"What if I don't do it?" he countered.

"Oh, you're going to do it. The question is how much pain and aggravation you'll go through to get it done. You belong to me until you're eighteen. I decide if you're going to the eighth grade or repeating the seventh grade. You can be the only seventeen-year-old in the seventh grade. It's your choice, Stephen. It makes no difference to me how long you take. You will finish. I suggest you get started." With that, Ms. Christian returned to her office and shut the door. Stephen looked at Ms. Coty, who shook her head.

"A word to the wise," she said, "she's mad. My advice is to write. You'll do what she wants, so you may as well get it done." She turned and resumed her typing.

* * *

At four-thirty, Stephen was both hungry and about to wet his pants. Ms. Christian left her office with her pocketbook. Stephen was sitting, holding his hand. The third finger on his right hand had an indention and was red. He knew that indention was permanent, a reminder of who was responsible for his actions. His thumb, index finger, and middle finger throbbed. Stephen smirked. He figured his mother could sue the school and get a bunch of money for his pain and suffering.

Ms. Christian came over to the desk and picked up the pad. Stephen didn't look up at her. She methodically turned page after page, scanning the page numbers and every line. Stephen squirmed in his seat. He had to pee badly.

Finally, Ms. Christian looked at Stephen and said, "You're finished. I excuse you. In case you're wondering, the next time you're removed from a class and sent to my office, there will be two tablets. Now go."

Stephen scrambled out of the desk and headed to the bathroom.

* * *

The man couldn't stand the smell of himself. It didn't matter; he wouldn't have to smell himself much longer. The park was his special place. He enjoyed coming here when he could after work, sometimes in the early morning before work, and on the weekends. The weekends were the most fun. Getting to the park early, he would claim his bench before anyone else got it. Rachel, his wife, often joined him at noon with a picnic lunch. They'd talk and watch the people and the lake. He looked over his left shoulder at the bench's inscription plate:

A PEACEFUL PLACE IN A CHALLENGED WORLD

RALPH BIXNER

9/15/2001

It had cost him ten thousand dollars for the right to have that plaque placed on this bench. He had selected this bench on this path because it was one of the least-used walkways in the park. The solitude helped him relax when he was here, and no one came by. He found peace in just watching the lake ripple in the breeze or watching the ducks glide by on the water. He could, or used to, read a book, listen to classical piano concertos on his AirPods, or just watch the squirrels or birds scurry around looking for food. In the beginning, both would come over, expecting him to drop some crumbs or pieces of his sandwich. But that wasn't his style. His philosophy was everyone for themselves. He had made it to the top, or at least close enough to enjoy the rarefied air at the top. Everybody else could do the same without his help. Then it happened.

Sitting on this bench, reading a book and sipping some water, he looked up. It was as if the entire world changed. He took no pleasure from the sights before him. The lake was dirty, with trash around the shoreline. Litter was in the grass. The bridge was rusty and its paint was peeling. He didn't know how he had thought the place was beautiful.

The next day, he didn't get out of bed. He called his office and told his assistant he was sick. He'd be back in three days. The second day, he realized something was wrong and called his doctor.

Clinical depression, the doctor had said. No problem, he went on, just take these pills.

It'd been six months, and he was still walking around in a fog. The pills got his body out of the bed, but his mind stayed negative and out of touch. He'd had enough of the doctor and the shrink the doctor had sent him to. Just what his childhood had to do with him now, at sixty-four and depressed, escaped him. All he knew for sure was at two hundred fifty dollars an hour, he would remain depressed if he had to write those checks. He took a leave of absence from his job. He didn't need the money. His entire life, he'd been both frugal and lucky with his investments. He had plenty of money to last a lifetime, no matter how short or long that lifetime would be. He stopped seeing the shrink and threw the pills into the storm sewer. Only as he watched them disappear did he realize he could have sold them to some street junkie. Not thinking about selling the pills was a symptom of his current state of mind, and, likewise, realizing he could have made money from them was a sign he was hanging on to the ledge of sanity by his fingertips.

He'd been on the bench since four o'clock. His right hand was in his jacket pocket, wrapped around a Smith & Wesson AirLite .357 magnum revolver. The internet had said a .22 would do the job, but he wanted to be sure. In his depressed state, he didn't want to do it half-assed. That'd be the ultimate depressing situation. He looked around. No one was paying any attention to him. He palmed the gun with his hand and slipped it out of his coat pocket, moving his hand to the inside of his jacket, over his heart. The thought of disfiguring his head bothered him. He didn't want to be messy, just get the job done quickly and painlessly. Closing his eyes, he eased his finger onto the trigger. He turned the muzzle toward his heart. His finger squeezed the trigger, taking up the slack used as a safety, until the trigger gave resistance. Squeezing his eyes tight, he took a deep breath. A thud sounded and the bench vibrated, startling him. His finger released the trigger, and his eyes shot open. He saw a kid sitting at the opposite end of the bench. God damn, he thought. What's that kid doing here? I've got to get rid of him.

Stephen didn't want to get home before his mother arrived since he'd have to watch his younger brother and sister if he did. Mrs. Gonzales could keep them. He saw the man on the bench, but all the other benches were full. Stephen dropped his backpack between the man and himself and plopped down on the far edge.

"Kid, run along. I'm expecting someone any moment," Ralph said, keeping his hand and the gun under his jacket, over his heart.

Stephen looked at him and crinkled his nose. "You run along. What are you, homeless or something?" he retorted.

"Or something. Look, kid, just move. I was here first. Get out of here."

"I don't want to leave, and you can't make me. I need to think things out, and this is as good a place as any." Stephen put his hand up to his face and squeezed his nose.

"Well, well—a smartass. Screw you, punk. Pissants like you are worthless. I tell you what: I can solve any problems you have, no matter what they are, by answering three questions you ask me. You ask the three questions, and if I don't solve all your problems, I'll give you fifty bucks to leave."

People had called Stephen worse, but not on a day when his mother had turned her back on him and his principal had brutalized him and forced him to realize he was the reason he was failing in school. His eyes glistened with tears, his chin quivered, and he quickly turned away so the man wouldn't see him cry.

"What's the matter? You afraid I'll solve all your problems, or are you so rich you don't need the money?"

"I don't want your money. You wouldn't look and smell like you do if you had fifty dollars," Stephen said as he wiped his eyes on the sleeve of his shirt.

"Well, you're a smartass and a dumbass." Ralph palmed the AirLite and quickly put it in his right jacket pocket. He then reached back into his inside left breast pocket and pulled out his wallet, extracted a fifty-dollar bill, and held it up for Stephen to see. "Now, you satisfied I have fifty dollars to give you?"

Stephen looked at the man and the money. "Okay, here's your first question: why doesn't my mother love me?" He choked on the last two words.

Ralph looked at Stephen. He hadn't expected that question. "That's easy to answer," he said. "Tell me about your father."

"I don't have a father."

"He dead or divorced from your mother?"

"I don't know. I just know he left right before my little sister was born."

"How many brothers and sisters do you have?"

"A brother, nine, and a sister, five."

"Anybody around to help your mother out?"

"No. It's just the four of us."

"Who helps with the younger kids?"

"A neighbor lets them into the apartment when I'm delayed at school."

"What do you mean, 'delayed at school'?"

Stephen looked down at his shoes. "You know: having to go to detention."

"Does your mother work?"

"Yeah, she works as a stock person in a grocery store."

"What hours does she work?"

"Eight to six are her regular hours, but if she can get some overtime, she takes it."

"What, five days a week?"

"No, six days a week, regular. If she gets the overtime, it's on Sunday afternoon."

"Who fixes dinner for all of you?"

"She does."

"Who cleans up the apartment? Who gives all of you a bath?"

"She does."

"On Saturday, do you watch the younger kids?"

"No, she pays Mrs. Gonzales to watch them."

"All right. I'll first answer your question with a question, and then give you the answer to your question. Why should your mother love you? While you think about that, think about this as well: Your father walked out on your mother. She could have turned you and your brother and sister over to the Department of Children and Family Services to be split up and placed in foster homes. She could have been like your father and enjoyed a carefree life instead of working six, sometimes six and a half days a week, for barely enough money to get by on. That would have been more fun for a young lady than trying to raise three children alone. Now, if you were in your mother's shoes, how would you feel if your oldest son didn't care enough for you and his brother and sister to help by taking care of the children after school, making sure they were safe and doing their homework, so she wouldn't have to pay the neighbor—what's her name?"

"Gonzales."

"Yeah, that's it. So, she wouldn't have to spend precious money making sure her children were safe while she worked? You know, if you look at it, I'd say your mother must love the three of you more than she loves anything, including her own life. When she's at work, she knows the only thing standing between her and her three children being homeless is that job. What would you do?" Ralph stared at Stephen. He knew how much courage it took for Stephen to ask the question and how brutal his answer had been. It needed to be brutal. This kid had to leave so he could get on with his plan.

Stephen looked off at the lake and a gaggle of Canada geese pecking the grass along the bank. One gander was standing outside the gaggle, its head moving in all directions, alert to any potential predator. He sat quietly for a couple of minutes.

He then turned to the man and said, "You think you're so smart, tell me why nobody at school likes me."

"Jeez, I thought you had tough questions for me. I'll answer again with a question and the answer you don't want to hear. What have you done to be a friend to anyone? If you want friends, you must be a friend. You're in school. Evidently, you're a distraction to your classmates and the teachers since you get detention a lot. Have you ever thought about how that makes school more difficult for the teachers, who must deal with you instead of teaching? What kind of mood do you think they're in after your disruption? How can the other kids keep up with their learning when you're depriving them of their time to hear the lessons and ask questions? School might seem like a waste of time for you, but—what grade are you in?"

"Seventh."

"Yeah, that's the smartass grade. You probably have an A-plus in Smartass 101. Anyway, unless you want to be in a gang of losers, school is important. You see that building over there?" Ralph pointed to the San Ramo towers.

"Yeah," Stephen said.

"You live there?"

"Don't be stupid," Stephen snapped.

"Listen, I'm not the stupid one here, smartass. You think any of the guys who own those apartments are high-school dropouts? Hell, no. They knew they printed the ticket to success in school. Every grade is important as the foundation for the next. If you don't live there, where do you live?"

"Hamilton House."

"The projects. I guess you want to stay in that roach-infested place, right? You don't want a chance to move over to the San Ramo or some other classier building, right? If you want friends, you're going to make the right ones in school. Now they know you as a cutup and a disrupter. So, you'll have to show them first that you've changed.

"Don't look glum; that's an easy fix. Starting tomorrow, you show up and pay attention. Have your homework done. Ask questions if you don't know something. You know why asking questions is important? Because if you don't know what the teacher is teaching, nine out of ten times, the other kids don't either. They're just too scared to show their ignorance. You ask the question, and you become the leader. You become the leader, and you end up with plenty of friends. Help your classmates be better students and you won't ever be without friends. One more question and the fifty is yours, and then you can run along and leave me in peace."

Stephen sat quietly. The man said he needed the courage to ask questions to make friends. Well, he may as well start now. Besides, he won't answer this question, and the fifty dollars would go a long way. He might even give his mother part of it. He turned again and looked at the man. "If you're so smart, why are you sitting on this bench, smelling like a goat and looking like a bum?"

Ralph looked at the boy and was dumbstruck by the question. How could he tell a thirteen-year-old about depression? Ralph suddenly heard himself speaking. He knew it was his voice, but he didn't know where the words were coming from.

"All my life, kid, I wanted to succeed. I wasn't an A student, just a C-plus, but I gave it all I had. Year after year I took myself to the limit, building the habit of doing my best. I'll tell you a secret, kid. Once you get out of high school, if you've built the habit of doing your absolute best at everything, your success accelerates as you get older. That building I pointed out to you is where I live. Twentieth floor, eleven rooms, overlooking the park. One day I was sitting right here on this bench, and the world suddenly turned black."

"Black?"

"A figure of speech, kid. I couldn't see the beauty of the world anymore. There no longer was a purpose in my life. I couldn't understand why I was alive. All the material riches meant nothing. Hell, I have a good wife and three grown and wonderful children. I couldn't find pleasure in them anymore. My wife, at my urging, went to our condo in Miami last month. If she was around, I was afraid I would say something hurtful. I had hurt her enough these past few months.

"I learned something today. Whatever my problems are, other people are carrying just as heavy a burden as I am. My challenges aren't insurmountable at all. You should listen to what I have to say because it will shorten your path to success and sweeten your enjoyment of life every step of the way. Most of all, you'll protect yourself from the blackness by making sure you help someone every day. Here. Here's your fifty dollars. If you want to, share it with your mother, who loves you more than you'll ever realize until you become a parent."

Stephen reached out, took the money, and put it in his shirt pocket. "This is a nice spot. You come here often?"

Ralph looked at him and took a minute to answer. "Yeah. That's my name on the plaque. I come here a lot."

"Well, maybe I'll see you in the future."

"What time do you get out of school, smartass? When you don't screw up and have detention?"

"Three o'clock."

"I tell you what: I'll be here tomorrow until three fifteen. If you get out on time, I'd like to hear how your day went and what you have for homework. If you get detention, I won't be here when you arrive. I don't have time for cutups."

"Maybe I'll see you tomorrow."

"What's your name, smartass?"

"Stephen. Stephen Elwood. What's yours?"

"Ralph Bixner."

"My mom doesn't let me go out without a bath each day."

"Yeah, I hear you, Stephen. Smart woman."

"See you around." Stephen picked up his backpack, slung it over his shoulder, and headed down the path. Ralph watched him go.

"Hey, Stephen!" Ralph called out.

Stephen turned and looked back.

"Thanks."

Be Careful What You Pray For

HENRY LOOKED AT HIS watch: eight-fifteen. He was happily waiting. She was in the confessional with Father Damien. A strikingly attractive woman in her mid-fifties, as religious as she was, was worth waiting for. She was going to his apartment for the first time. They would have breakfast and then go strolling through the Ramble in Central Park until it was time for a late lunch. Maybe they wouldn't get to the park.

They would. His apartment would disappoint her, but he would make sure she knew it was temporary. What he liked about her was her holiness. She wouldn't hop into bed with him after only six weeks. She would expect more. He would give her more—a lot more. The duffel bag could buy a lifetime of more. At least for his lifetime. These had been the happiest six weeks of the last two-and-a-half years, and she was the reason.

* * *

It all began when he stopped at a red light at Stafford and Exeter in Chicago. Life was calm. His wife had died four months before, and he'd fallen into a depression, a state of mind unknown to him. He and Helen had spent forty years together. He was twenty-one and she was seventeen when they stood in front of the priest. Both virgins, both in love. He was to die first, but God forgot to tell the cancer. His name was Carl. His childhood friend was his boss. After Helen died, he went to Mickey and told him he wanted to retire. Mickey told him to take a break; he was just depressed over losing Helen.

Carl and Mickey grew up together, going to the same schools and living within two blocks of each other as kids. At eighteen they graduated from high school together and went out to conquer the world together—at least their vision of the world. Mickey was the leader because he could see the big picture, while Carl understood the details were important.

Carl married Helen in a double ceremony with Mickey and Shelia. Father Bede understood that these two lifelong friends wanted to share their auspicious day. The two couples found townhouses on the same block in their old neighborhood and raised their families together. Helping one another bury their parents when the cycle of life required it, they grieved together. They celebrated together when their children graduated from high school, went off to college, got married, and moved far from the old neighborhood. When the grandchildren came along, Carl was the godfather of Mickey's and Mickey was the godfather of Carl's. Then Helen got the big C. Mickey and Shelia were by Carl and Helen's side during the chemo treatments, the many operations, the searches for a realistic-looking wig, and the trips to O'Malley's for greasy, high-calorie hamburgers, fries, and milkshakes to retard Helen's weight loss as she slowly wasted away. Then the ordeal was over. Mickey and Shelia held Carl, and the three of them cried as they watched the coffin being lowered into the ground. Each dropped a single yellow rose and a handful of dirt on the mahogany and brass box holding Helen's body.

The day Helen went to heaven, Carl realized he would not qualify to follow her to that peaceful, everlasting place. He was beside himself with grief over losing her and the certainty of never joining her. He went to see Father Bede in the confessional. The priest explained to Carl how he could bend the arc of his life so he could be with his beloved when his time came. Father Bede explained to Carl about God's unconditional forgiveness of sin. If a person truly repents for past transgressions and then dies, God will welcome the person into everlasting love and happiness in His world. That was when Carl went to Mickey, and Mickey suggested giving his grief some time. Time did not help. Carl went back to Mickey and pleaded for the right to retire. Mickey relented. Carl was happy. He and Father Bede charted a course for Carl that would assure his entrance into the Kingdom of God alongside his beloved Helen. That was when the accident happened.

The car slammed into the back of Carl's Lexus with enough force to push the car a third of the way into the intersection.

Not hurt, Carl's anger was his focus. Turning off the engine, he got out, holding his neck just in case the driver who hit him had decent insurance. The other driver got out of his car and was looking at the damage when Carl walked up.

"Gee, I'm sorry," the driver said, not identifying himself. Carl heard sirens approaching. In less than a minute, an ambulance pulled up and so did a tow truck. Carl realized something was amiss but didn't comprehend what was happening. The ambulance rear doors opened, and a paramedic disembarked.

The paramedic came over to Carl and said: "Carl O'Brien, you are under arrest for the murders of Joey Esposito and Billy Aliffi."

"I want my lawyer," Carl quickly said.

"Mr.O'Brien, don't say another word. Get in the ambulance and sit quietly." The paramedic nodded at the driver of the other car and got back in the ambulance, which took off with sirens screaming and lights flashing. On the way to the hospital, they put a neck brace on Carl and placed him on a stretcher. At the hospital, Carl went in, bypassing the ER and going directly to a fourth-floor room. In the room were three men he had never seen before. They identified themselves as officials of the U.S. Justice Department's Organized Crime Unit and were there to ask him one multiple-choice question. What did he want: (A) thirty years without possibility of parole in the Colorado Supermax prison, or (B) the Witness Program for telling all he knew about Mickey and Mickey's bosses and associates?

Carl's indecision about his choices lasted for thirty minutes while the Justice Department officials conferred to discuss his demands: a new face, immunity and a new life in the city of his choice, a regular social security check for the rest of his life in his new name, and the duffel bag and its contents that he kept hidden in his home's basement. They said yes to all stipulations, and Carl spent the next five months talking into a tape recorder and appearing in courtrooms. Mickey went to Supermax for thirty years with no possibility of parole, his crew all got five to fifteen years in Leavenworth, and his bosses continued enjoying their country club lifestyle and their second homes in Florida.

Carl became Henry. He got a new nose, chin, and hair color. He grew a beard that he kept trimmed and dyed like the young guys in the magazines. The feds set him up with a furnished second-floor walk-up in Brooklyn and paid for a year's rent in advance. Carl, now Henry, stayed for one week. They deposited his monthly social security check straight into a bank account, which he could access from anywhere in the country. His debit card would give him access when he wanted it. Otherwise, the money would build up. When he left Brooklyn, Henry left his clothes, his shoes, and everything but the duffel bag.

He ended up in Spanish Harlem on One Hundred Seventh Street and First Avenue. He went to several thrift shops and bought the basic essentials in clothes and needed items. His newly furnished apartment was in a rodent-infested building. It was a third-floor walk-up with a sitting room, kitchenette, bathroom, and bedroom. Trash littered the stairways and landing on the third floor. There was a single uncovered light bulb on each flight of stairs and one in the middle of the third-floor landing. A pawn shop occupied the first floor. The front of the building had two features Henry liked. First was the fire escape. Each floor had a level grate stretching across several windows, including Henry's sitting-room window. It was possible to sit on a bucket balanced across the metal rods making up the fire escape floor, catching a breeze and watching the people going about their necessary movements to survive on very little in an expensive city. From this perch, the second reason Henry chose this apartment was the view of St. Anne's Holy Roman Catholic Church steeple.

Carl, now Henry, had not forgotten that his current goals in life were to make amends for his past transgressions and to be with his beloved Helen in heaven. He knew the way to ensure he achieved his aim was to take part in the Catholic faith.

St. Anne's was perfect. It was a poor, dying parish church with a single priest in his fifties. Henry went to the seven o'clock morning Mass every day of the week except Sunday, when he went to the eight o'clock Mass since there was none at seven. He engaged the priest after each service. Three weeks after arriving, he made an appointment to see Father Damien for confession and a counseling session. The parishioners called him Father D and loved him. They knew they were lucky to have a man of such high intellect and education as their pastor. They believed God had blessed them because they were so attentive to their religion. It didn't take Henry long to understand that Father D was fond of children and bourbon, not necessarily in that order. The priest used the bourbon to keep his other urges in check. He was, however, brilliant and learned in the church's dogma and what it takes to get into heaven. That's all Henry wanted from a priest: knowledge of the path to the Kingdom of God and his Helen.

After only a month, Henry was substituting as altar server at the daily seven o'clock Mass when the only altar boy either overslept or just didn't want to serve that day. The first time Henry put on the cassock and surplice; he could hardly contain his joy. He knew he was on the way to redemption.

Henry's life was complete. He was in a safe place where even the Feds couldn't find him, leading a life of communion with God and atonement. An 860-acre peaceful park was a few short blocks away for his enjoyment. There he could spend his waking hours, never tiring or getting bored, enjoying the natural beauty while watching the people of New York at play. He'd stay in the park every day until the sun faded away over the Hudson River. At least he thought life was complete.

Henry never expected to think of another woman after Helen. He was unique in his line of work. He and Helen were virgins when they married and neither became intimate with anyone else during their life together. One beautiful, clear Wednesday morning, Henry was acting as altar server. When it came time for the Eucharist, Henry held the wine chalice in his hands with a napkin across his right forearm, standing alongside Father D passing out communion wafers. A woman who appeared to be in her mid-fifties waited patiently, her eyes almost closed, her hands pressed together with the fingers extended and silver rosary beads intertwined among them. Her mouth moved silently as she said the rosary to only God and herself. After taking the wafer on her tongue, she stepped sideways, so she was standing in front of Henry. She raised her brown eyes to him, and his heart skipped a beat. If one look could communicate piousness, she had it. She never moved her eyes away from his, even as she took the chalice from him, sipped the wine, and returned the cup to his trembling hands. Removing the napkin from his arm, she touched her lips and replaced the napkin. She turned, bowed her head, and went back to her seat.

After Mass, Henry disrobed in the sacristy and went out to the nave from behind the altar. The woman was still in the pew, silently saying the rosary. Henry genuflected in front of the altar and walked down to where she was kneeling.

"Good morning," he said in a low tone.

"Good morning," she replied.

"I'm Henry. Do you come here often?"

"I'm new to the city and parish. I've lived most of my life in the south."

"What is your name?"

"Rachael. Rachael Santiago."

"As I've said, I'm Henry. Henry Williamson."

"I'm so happy I found St. Anne's. You can feel God is present in this church."

"Yes, you're right. Do you have time for breakfast?"

"Thank you, but no. I have a job interview to go to."

"Perhaps another time. Do you live around here?"

"Yes, six blocks from here."

"Well, have a nice day. I hope the job interview goes well. I'm sure we will see each other again," he said, smiling and turning to walk out of the church.

Henry didn't see Rachael again until Sunday Mass. Since he wasn't serving, he went over, genuflected, and sat next to her. Both went to communion.

When Mass was over, he turned to her and said, "I'm going to have a sandwich in Central Park and stay for a while. Would you care to join me?"

"Yes, that would be nice," Rachael said, slipping her rosary beads into her purse.

They walked together comfortably and talked mostly about the neighborhood. Moments of silence seemed natural, not like forced dead air. Henry steered them to the Trustee Gardens at One Hundred Fifth Street and Fifth Avenue.

"Do you come to the park often?"

"I come to the park every day and stay all day."

"You don't work?"

"No. I'm retired." He thought for a minute. "I retired early. Perhaps too early. Did you get the job?"

"I don't understand," Rachael said, looking at him.

"Last Wednesday, after Mass, you said you had a job interview. That's why you couldn't have breakfast."

"Oh, no. I mean, they haven't decided yet. I'm in the running, though. Pray I get it."

"Yes, I will. What type of job is it?"

"Uh, essentially a secretarial position."

"How long have you been in the city?"

"Just one month. How long have you been here?" Rachael asked quickly.

"A couple of years."

"Do you live near St. Anne's?"

"Yeah, about three blocks away."

"Do you work?"

"No. I'm retired on medical disability."

"Yes, you just told me that. How silly of me to ask again. What did you do?"

"Jack of all trades. Mostly residential renovations. That's how I hurt my back. Here we are. Have you been here before?" Henry asked as he showed her the archway for the Trustee Gardens.

Rachael stepped through the arch and looked at the fountain on the other end of the lawn. Behind the fountain was an elevated arbor covered in wisteria vines, with stairways on each end.

"It's beautiful," Rachael said, grabbing his arm. Henry had always enjoyed his delight in the Trustee Gardens, but the emotions he felt when she touched his arm sent his pride off the charts as he introduced her to this lovely spot.

"Come, let's have a seat over in the shade on the walkway. Are you hungry? I have a home-made sub sandwich. It's on a hard, crusty French baguette. I prefer that bread to the soft type used in sandwich shops."

"Oh, I couldn't. You won't have enough for yourself."

"Sure I will. If Jesus could feed the multitudes with two loaves and fishes, you and I can share a sub sandwich."

"You're so kind. Thank you. I can't stay long, but thank you. You're so kind."

An hour later Henry sat on the same bench, his eyes closed, reliving every moment of the morning. He hadn't felt this way since his beloved Helen had died. How old was Rachael? He guessed mid-fifties. That was close to the same age Helen would have been. They had the same smile—mysterious and mischievous. Rachael's eyes were both sad and sparkling. Helen's were the same. Helen's sadness came from knowing his line of work. Why were Rachael's sad? Rachael was Hispanic. Helen was Irish. Night and day. Wasn't night and day part of the same twenty-four-hour period? He knew everything about Helen, and he wanted to know everything about Rachael. He didn't know her favorite color. What was her favorite type of music? Did she like movies? What books did she read? Did she like the first Pope from Latin America? Henry was alive with curiosity, and he reveled in the feeling.

He stopped short in his thinking. He realized the spartan existence he had developed was not conducive to an open relationship with someone. What if she asked him the same questions about what he liked? What would he say? Was he betraying his beloved Helen by having these feelings? Henry realized he needed to speak to Father Damien. What he knew for certain was he did not want to stray from the narrow path leading to heaven. Father Damien would know the boundaries. Yes, he needed to speak to the padre.

Henry and Rachael saw each other at Mass the following Wednesday. She excitedly told him she had gotten the secretarial job at Hugo's auto repair and salvage yard. She couldn't go to the park that day, but she could the following Sunday. Henry beamed with happiness.

"I'll bring us a picnic lunch," she said, touching his arm.

On Sunday, they went to the Ramble rather than the Trustee Gardens. Henry led her through the maze of paths to a gazebo on the edge of the lake. They had the spot all to themselves. Rachael opened her large purse and extracted two single-serving-size Tupperware bowls filled with a salad and strips of ham, two small glass cups, and a Swell bottle of iced tea. She'd brought each of them a metal fork.

"You didn't have to go to such an elaborate meal," Henry said.

"It's nothing. I don't believe in disposable items when it's so easy to wash the dishes and fork. Besides, you deserve only the best," she said, smiling.

Their relationship fell into a routine. They would see each other at Mass on Wednesday before she went to work and on Sunday when she would have a picnic lunch for them. Each week he would select a unique part of the park for the picnic and surprise her. Henry thought more and more of her and less of his beloved Helen. His guilt grew, so he made another appointment to speak to Father Damien.

The two men sat in the rectory study, with shelves of books lining each wall, two old and cracked green leather chairs, and a small Victorian turned-leg table between the chairs. On the table was a fifth of Jim Beam bourbon, a bowl of ice, and two half-full glasses.

"Father, my Helen was—no, *is* the only woman I have ever loved, both physically and spiritually. Now I'm having some feelings for a woman I met at Mass. I'm confused. I feel like I'm betraying Helen," Henry lamented before sipping his Jim Beam.

"Henry, God has given each of us the nature to love deeply. It is a gift from our loving Father. When we lose the one we love, we experience grief in the same magnitude of the joyous love we experienced. Most people don't understand this equality of emotional balance. Grief, the demonstration of our loss and sorrow, is God's way to cauterize the heart and soul, preparing both for healing and for accepting happiness and love again. Your Helen has been in heaven for how long?" Father Damien said before draining his glass, reaching for two cubes of ice, and pouring another half glass of bourbon.

"Two-and-a-half years."

"You have missed her dearly all that time, right?"

"Yes, Father. My world ended when she died. If I hadn't known without a doubt that I would go directly to hell, I would have ended my life then."

"I suspected as much from your constant questioning about death and the path for assuring your entrance into heaven. From what you have told me, you are leading the life of a monk, praying and preparing for the day you can go to heaven. And now, Henry, you are awakening to the beauty of the birds singing, the fragrance of the flowers, and the laughter of humans, all through the kindness and attention of this woman."

"Yes, Father, exactly. That's my dilemma. Rachael is a striking woman. She is as devout as my Helen was. Her eyes have the same sadness and elegance as my Helen's eyes. Yes, Father, I feel alive for the first time in two-and-a-half years and want to pursue this devout woman and see if we can build a life together. Is that wrong? Is that a betrayal of Helen?"

"Henry, I'm confident your Helen would want you to be happy during the time you have left in this world. Building a blessed life with this woman who loves God as much as you do will not cause you to deviate from your path to heaven when the Lord calls."

"You really think so, Father?"

"Yes, I do, Henry. God understands a physical relationship between a devout husband and wife is natural, even looked upon as special since the two partners assist each other in keeping the focus on God in this secular world. Because you are so committed to God's path, I'm confident He sent—what's her name again?"

"Rachael. Rachael Santiago."

"—to you until your time to go to the Kingdom of God arrives."

"Thank you, Father. It's comforting to have your perspective."

Saturday afternoon Henry returned from the park shortly after lunch. There was work to be done. He entered his building and noted the trash, papers, used needles, condoms, empty broken bottles, and old newspapers on the stairs, along with the dirt leading up to the third landing. On the landing was more of the same. He couldn't do anything about the peeling paint and chipped plaster, but he could clean the place up. Entering his apartment, he looked at the sitting room. Scattered about were newspapers, magazines, and takeout food wrappers. A stain on the sofa and it's worn fabric from age and laying a greasy head back while napping would not do. He needed a throw cover for it. He straightened the shade on the floor lamp and turned the ripped part toward the wall. Moving on to the kitchenette, he began throwing away old paper dishes. An overflowing trash can, counters sticky with spilt food, and the few dishes he owned sitting dirty in the sink greeted him. He moved to the bathroom and looked at the dirt rings around the tub, the toilet, and the sink. He noticed the iron rust stains in all three. Finally, he moved to the bedroom where the double bed had torn, dirty sheets. There was no spread or blanket. A straight-backed wooden chair was the only other furniture in the room. His few clothes hung in the closet. Dirty clothes were obscuring the duffel bag on the closet floor.

Returning to the kitchen, Henry found a pencil in a drawer, ripped a page from a magazine, and made a list. Back in the bedroom, he uncovered the duffel bag, took out a plastic bag with hundred-dollar bills inside, and extracted six of them. He left the apartment.

His first trip was to the hardware store, where he bought trash bags, a mop, a broom, a dustpan, a bucket, and all the other items he needed to clean the stairs, landing, and apartment. Two hours later, his second trip was to the furniture and dry goods store around the corner. There he bought a small table and throw rug for the bedroom, a lamp, a shower curtain and matching toilet seat cover for the bathroom, a sofa shawl for the back of the sofa to cover the stains and worn areas, a throw rug for the sitting room floor, and a coffee table to go in front of the sofa. For the kitchen, he bought a four-place setting of plastic dishes, cups, and glasses. He bought four metal knives, forks, and spoons. Finally at eight, he went to the corner bodega and bought ingredients for breakfast the next day.

When he had done all he could to make his apartment presentable, he sat on the sofa and realized how far he had spiraled down. Whose fault was it? Helen's for dying? Of course not. The government for forcing him into the deal he'd made? No. They gave him no proper choice, but a choice, nonetheless. He realized he was the reason for this state he was in. Not twenty feet away was enough money for him to live a good life for a long time. Tomorrow, if he brought Rachael back here for breakfast, he would make sure she knew this was a temporary place. He would think of an excuse. Maybe, just maybe, she would have breakfast here and stay instead of going to the park. The thought sent chills through his body.

* * *

"Henry, thank you for waiting for me. This is such a wonderful idea: to have breakfast at your apartment. I don't think I've ever had a man cook for me." They walked, holding hands, down York Street. It was a beautiful day: blue sky, steady breeze off the East River, and children playing in their Sunday clothes. "Do we need to stop at the store and buy some ingredients?"

"No, I have everything we'll need. Please understand, this is only a temporary place until I find something nicer. I want to be close to St. Anne's, and this was the only place available when I came to the city."

"Henry, if it's yours, I'm sure it's nice."

When they arrived, Rachael complimented Henry on the apartment's cleanliness as she walked from room to room, careful not to touch anything. In the bedroom, she moved the dirty clothes with her foot and saw the duffel bag. She moved the clothes back into place. Henry was working diligently in the kitchen, preparing the Spanish omelet, toast, and juice. He had already set two places on the coffee table in the living room.

Breakfast was a success. "Henry, your wife was so lucky before she passed to have a husband who could cook like this."

"Thank you, but she wouldn't let me in the kitchen until she got sick."

"How long were you married?"

"Forty years."

"A long life together. You must miss her."

"I do, except that in the last several weeks, I've found joy again."

"Really? How is that?" Rachael said, her head tilted down but her eyes looked at him and penetrated his.

"Because of you. I didn't believe I would ever find another beautiful woman who loved God as much as I do and will enjoy the small things in life the way I do." Henry watched her reaction to his comment intently, trying to determine whether she felt as he did.

"I've had much unhappiness in my life, but God has always been there to comfort me when times were tough. I never thought I would find a man like you, someone who truly loves God as much as I do and enjoys the simple life. Perhaps God brought us together."

As they sat on the sofa, Rachael moved closer to Henry and put her head on his chest. He put his right arm around her. She leaned into him, and with her right hand unbuttoned his shirt. She slipped her hand into his shirt and caressed his chest, finding the breastbone.

"Henry, I hope we can always enjoy special moments like this," she said.

Henry tilted his head down and kissed her hair. He laid his head back on the sofa and closed his eyes. She removed her hand from his chest and unbuttoned her blouse, extracting an ice pick from the front of her bra. Henry felt a sting as she drove the ice pick into his chest, just below the breastbone and up into his heart. The sting became excruciating pain as she moved the pick back and forth, lacerating the heart.

As he struggled to move, she leaned in harder and said, "Mickey sends his regards, Carl." Henry stopped moving.

The Organ Grinder

"NO, SIR, BABY DIDN'T mean to.

"Yes, sir, you can take our picture if you want to. Let me put Baby's uniform on first.

"Huh? I've been with the carnival for twenty-five years. I've got a pin from Mr. Irby to show for it. Oh, Mr. Irby is the owner of the carnival. It's ten-karat gold plated and so nice. I wear it on special occasions. The rest of the time I keep it hidden here in my trailer.

"Why hidden? Goodness, a carny is just like the rest of the world—there are some really good people in the troop and some not so good. Like I said, that pin is ten-karat gold plated, but even more important than that, it's proof I've been an important part of this carnival, which is the best carny around.

"No, sir, I'm not from around here. I'm from Kansas, born and raised a Jayhawk in East Plains, Kansas. Have you ever heard of it? I didn't think so. It was a teeny-weeny town of

1,856 when I left. Daddy was the richest man in town. Yes, sir, the richest. We lived in a big three-story red brick house just outside of town, on Daddy's farm.

"Brothers and sisters? Yes, sir. I have four brothers and one sister. I'm the baby in the family. My sister, the next oldest, is seven years older than me. Daddy used to say I was a mistake, and my brothers and sister used to call me Mistake. I really didn't mind, I guess. The only thing I wish was they hadn't done it at school cause all the kids used to call me that too. But that doesn't matter. Now Momma and Daddy are dead, and my four brothers and their wives and families and my sister, her husband, and family all have houses on the farm. No, sir, it's not crowded cause there are three-thousand acres of planted land, and I don't know how many acres of trees, but there are a lot.

"No, sir, Daddy wasn't born rich. He made it all himself.

"What's that? How? Daddy got to be the richest man in town by being kind to people. He started out when he was young—fourteen I think he used to say—working for the man who owned the general store. Mr. Arthur, the man who owned the store, had children, but they didn't want to work in the store. Daddy—he was an orphan—came to town and had no place to stay, so he stayed in a small space, out of the wind and rain, between the store's back door and the firewood box. Well, Mr. Arthur caught him early one morning. At first, he thought Daddy was trying to steal from him, but after talking to Daddy, he realized he was alone, poor, and hungry.

He offered Daddy a job and said he'd pay him fifty cents a day, which was good for Mr. Arthur because most people made at least a dollar a day. Daddy was so happy, so he started working in the store that day. He worked seven days a week, from six in the morning to nine at night. He worked hard. At first, Mr. Arthur told Daddy what to do. Mr. Arthur had him sweeping the floors, dusting the shelves, and restocking the shelves, but soon Mr. Arthur didn't have to tell Daddy anything. Each day, by the time Mr. Arthur got to the store, Daddy had everything going great.

"Am I boring you, Mr. Aly? Those are mighty fine cameras.

"No, sir, I won't look at the camera.

"Baby is fine, he's really relaxed.

"No, he's not heavy. Go on doing what you need to do. Baby doesn't mind you as long as you stay over there.

"Okay, I'll go on. I'm proud of Daddy, and I get carried away sometimes. Anyway, Daddy worked hard. By the time Mr. Arthur died, he wasn't even coming into the store at all. After the funeral, Daddy went up to Joey, Ann, and Claire—those are Mr. Arthur's children—and told them he was quitting the store and going to open his own store. Just like that. Lord, those children were beside themselves. They had been living off the store, so to speak, for years. They asked Daddy to reconsider. He told them he wouldn't leave if they'd sign the store over to him and agree for him to pay them a monthly amount for the next fifteen years. Well, they agreed to do it, and that's how Daddy got his start. The Arthur kids didn't like it, but there wasn't anything they could do without trying to run the store themselves.

"Once Daddy owned the store, he put in a feed-and-seed section and began selling everything farmers needed to raise their crops. He'd even finance them until harvest time at an interest rate lower than the bank. If they had a poor harvest, he wouldn't sue them and would still lend them the money they needed to plant the next spring. All he asked them to do was to pledge their farm against the loans. When the Depression came and the farmers couldn't pay, he didn't put them off their farm. He put the farms in his name but told them they could stay there. He was fair and told them if they made enough to pay the loan and the interest on the loan, he'd let them pay off the loan and get their farms back. They never did. As one farmer said, 'The interest was fair but high and was due every day, just like the sun coming up.' Daddy was even good to widows. He left them on their farms and went out each month to collect the rent. Mama didn't like it, but there wasn't nothing she could do about it because Daddy was Daddy.

"My name? Gabriel. Momma gave me that name. Momma was the only one who called me that. Daddy and my brothers and sister called me Mistake. They thought that was funny. Even at school, all the kids in my class started calling me Mistake. That wasn't so funny, but it was okay, I guess. Around the dinner table, I said little because I was so much younger. When I tried to tell them about what happened at my school, everybody just ignored me until Momma told them to hush, that I had something to say. Everybody got quiet, but what I had to say no longer seemed important, so they kind of chuckled and went back to ignoring me. That's okay because I got to hear what they were saying. I was learning all along about how to get around this, ignore that, and take advantage of things.

"As I got older, my favorite subject in school was geography. I knew all the continents, all the mountain ranges, and all the oceans and seas. Want me to name them? I still can.

"No? Okay, I'll stick with my story. When I was ten, Momma ordered me a globe, round like the earth is, from the National Geographic Society. That was something special. When I got that globe, after dinner when everyone went out on the porch, I'd go up to my room and just look at that globe and pretend I was somewhere else. I'd spin the globe, shut my eyes, and then stab it with my finger. Wherever I landed on the globe, I'd pretend I was talking to the people and seeing how they lived. Even if I stabbed the ocean, I'd look for the nearest land or island and pretend I was on a boat going there. Momma would come in and say, 'Gabriel, it's time for you to be in bed.' She'd sort of pick up my things. I'd put on my nightgown, and then she'd tuck me in and tell me how much she loved me and how much life offered me, and she'd encourage me to study hard in school so I could do whatever I wanted when I grew up. My bed was up against the outside wall because I had the small room—they called it the trunk room—and the window was where I could look out and see all the stars or the lightning when it was storming. I'd dream myself asleep, just thinking of all the places I wanted to go.

"No, sir, Mr. Aly, Baby will let you come closer. Now, Baby, Mr. Aly ain't going to hurt me. He's just going to take our picture. Come over slow, Mr. Aly.

"Now, where was I? Oh, yes, when I was twelve, just when little girls have that time of the month, if you know what I mean, I got sick on the inside. It turned out they had to take out my baby-making parts, so I could never have children. Momma cried and cried, but I thought little of it because I didn't feel like children were the nicest people in the world. The only time I ever saw Momma talk sharply and loudly to Daddy was when he said my not being able to have children was God paying them back for having me. Boy, it was like an explosion of a boiler that had too much pressure. She lit into him about a lot of things—collecting rent from widows, charging too much interest to farmers who owed him money, calling me a Mistake, and letting the children tease me about it. She got so red in the face, I thought she was going to die. They didn't talk for over a week. If I remember right, Daddy slept at the store for a while. Anyway, as I got older, all the boys in my class wanted to be my special friend. I thought it was because I was finally getting to look like a girl, but one of my girlfriends said it was because the boys wouldn't have to use a rubber since I couldn't get pregnant. Well, I fooled them. Momma had always told me that a girl shouldn't have a special friend until she married. None of those boys ever got to second base, much less got a home run, until Jimmy came to the farm.

"Who was Jimmy? He was the son of the migrant workers' overseer Daddy hired to bring in the winter wheat and prepare the land for corn planting. It was my senior year of high school. Jimmy, his dad and mom, and his brother and sister all lived in a two-room house on the farm, on the other side of the big barn and grain bins. I'd see Jimmy around at school and when he was helping his dad with chores on our farm. Jimmy never called me Mistake. When he said Gabriel real low and slow, I got all tingly inside. He listened to all of my ideas, always smiling, looking directly at me, and telling me all about the places his family had seen when they moved from farm to farm as the seasons changed. By this time, I could drive one of the farm's pickup trucks. I'd sneak out of my bedroom window at night and meet Jimmy at the mechanic's shed. We'd push a truck down the road a way and then start the engine. We'd ride around for a while, smoking cigarettes and, when he could bring one, splitting a beer. Then we'd find a place to park. I still remember the first night Jimmy became my special friend. We were special at least three times. I still get goose bumps thinking about it.

"One night in late May, Billy, one of my brothers, was out hunting deer with lights, which was out of season and illegal. He came out of the woods into the clearing where me and Jimmy parked. Back home, all the hunters used ways to trick the deer, hogs, or birds when they hunted. They didn't care if it was legal or fair. They thought it was manly to cheat. Billy went and told Daddy about me and Jimmy. Daddy fired Jimmy's father and gave them only one day to clear out of the county or he'd have Jimmy arrested for rape.

"I'd already decided that I was going to leave when I graduated from high school. I didn't have many friends since it's hard to be friends with someone who calls you Mistake. Anyway, I had worked at the store since I was in the seventh grade. Daddy didn't pay me much, but from what he paid me, he made me give 10 percent to the church, put 10 percent in a savings account, and use the rest for things I wanted. What he didn't know was I wanted to have money when I graduated, so I put 20 percent of what I made inside my sock doll Momma made for me when I was a little girl. You know what, Mr. Aly? I still have that sock doll. Yes, I do. It still has some money in it. Nobody would think to look there for money. Ain't I smart?

"I decided I'd leave the day after graduation but wouldn't tell anyone until the night of graduation. Momma had all my brothers, their wives and families, my sister, her husband, and her children for a graduation celebration with a hog-killing and a big dinner under the oak trees. Daddy, my brothers, and my sister had spent the night before and the day of graduation roasting the pig and making pies and a cake, so they were too busy to come to the graduation, but that was okay cause Momma was there. When she hugged me after I got my diploma, I told her I was leaving in the morning. She had tears in her eyes but said she understood.

"Later that night, when me and her were doing the dishes after dinner and all the rest of the family was out on the front porch, Momma went over to the pantry, pushed aside jars of fruit from last fall's canning, took down a faded flour box, and gave me the money she had hidden there. It was more than $150. She had made it baking pies and cakes for people over the years. She put the money in my hand and put both of her hands on my shoulders, holding me at arm's length. Looking me in the eye, she told me I was not a mistake. She purposely did it with Daddy at a time she was pretty sure she'd get pregnant. Momma wanted another baby because she felt so alone cause all my brothers and sister were just like my Daddy. She wanted someone she could love and who would love her. She told me to go as far as I could and not look back. Momma told me she was proud of me, and she said I could do anything I really wanted to do. Hugging me so hard I thought she would squeeze all the breath out of me, I knew she loved me as much as I loved her.

"Yes, sir, Mr. Aly, I'm coming to that.

"I got on the train the next morning and didn't get off until Chicago. Chicago was a big, dirty city. I was staying at the YWCA and going to church like Momma told me to, but I was thinking about Jimmy most of the time. In a few days, I got a job in a store, but I didn't like it none. After five months, the carny came to town. One of my girlfriends at the Y was from the country and we went, figuring it would remind us of the county fairs we used to go to when we were growing up. I realized as soon as I got a funnel cake and saw the lights, the midway, and the sideshows that carnival life was for me. That same night, I got Mr. Zack Irby, the owner and boss, to give me a job. Me and my friend went back to the Y that night and I packed my bag. Well, to be honest, all I had were two dresses, two sets of underwear, two pairs of shoes, my Bible, a picture of Momma, my sock doll, and my diary. The next day I started working.

"Zack—Mr. Irby, I mean—put me to work in a ticket booth. He let me bunk in with Jefferson, the clown, his wife, and their two girls. Zack is a lot like my Daddy. He owns all the trailers, and we all pay him rent. I love carny life. Even if he didn't pay me, I'd do it, but don't tell him that. I'm now the organ grinder, and Baby is my sidekick. How I got this job is another story for another time.

"Yes, sir. I'm going to explain what happened now. I haven't had a special friend in a while, a long while. Ralph, the father of the little people family in the sideshow, has had his eye on me for some time. I think it's because I'm so tall, have a nice figure, and smile at him whenever we meet. Anyway, two nights ago, Sara—that's Ralph's wife—was sick. Ralph, who had been flirting with me and 'accidentally' bumping into my breasts when he could, suggested he come over and visit. I put Baby to bed early, and when he was asleep, Ralph climbed in through the bedroom window. As I told you, it was a long time since I'd had a special friend. I was excited. He quietly took off my clothes, and then I undressed him. It pleasantly surprised me to see that little men aren't little everywhere, if you know what I mean. Ralph was standing on the bed, and I was kneeling on the bed. He had his hands on each side of my head while he was in my mouth. Well, as I told you, I was excited cause I hadn't had a special friend in a while, and I guess I just moaned louder than I should have. Baby woke up, looked at us, and must have thought Ralph was hurting me. Baby screeched, jumped up, and flew over and landed on Ralph. I jerked my head up, Ralph came out of my mouth, and I guess Baby just grabbed that part of Ralph and started pulling and scratching him. By the time I got Baby calmed down, all the carny trailers lights were on and people were banging on my trailer door.

"Yes, sir. Ralph gets out of the hospital tomorrow. No, sir, Sara's not mad at me. She says she's glad Ralph got what he deserved. Carny people are a family, no matter what. No, sir, they will do nothing to Baby. You're welcome. I hope the pictures come out really good."

The Quail Hunt

"DON'T SHOOT MY DOGS," our guide and dog handler Bo said, looking me in the eye as he handed me my gun, breech open, from the gun box on the back of the buggy. This wasn't the first insult I experienced that day. We were standing at the crossroads in the center, where the vast expanse of quail-hunting land stretched in all directions. We enjoyed the bluest of blue skies, with just a wisp of clouds passing over the wire-grass fields and telephone-pole-straight longleaf pine trees. There were two buggies, two guides, and four "guns"—that's what they called the hunters who were paying for the privilege of being embarrassed by two-ounce feather-covered jet engines.

Earlier I had driven up to the chain-link fence's electric gate, which barred access to the six-thousand-acre hunting plantation. Waiting on the inside with the gate opener in his truck, sat Johnny, an intern. Like so many young men raised in the rural south, he just wanted to be around hunting, even for only minimum wage. He opened the gate and pointed to a spot for me to park my car.

"Welcome to Estes Plantation," he said, reaching for my gun bag and coat. He placed these essentials in the back of his pickup. I opened the breech of my shotgun as I took it from my car's backseat. The gun rode in the cab between the two of us, still with the breech open.

Quail hunting, at least in the magazines and books today, is a gentlemen's experience. That's true in the southeast, where most of the typical hunting land is on private plantations. Outside the plantations, former quail land is being developed or used to cultivate row crops or orchards. It takes a serious amount of money every year to maintain a habitat conducive to quail. Most commercial hunting plantations do not have coveys of truly wild birds. They release birds raised at a farm devoted to quail sold to hunting plantations at the beginning of the season, a week before the particular hunt, or the morning of a hunt.

"Are these wild birds or kick-'em-up birds?" I asked Johnny curiously, still looking out the window at the plantation as we rode to the lodge. Released birds that preferred to run along the ground rather than fly inspired the negative name I used for pen-raised birds. It always seemed to me these may be the smartest birds since real hunters just can't bring themselves to shoot a bird running on the ground.

"They're released birds, but we put them out on Monday before a Saturday hunt, so they're acclimatized better than most released birds."

That's better than most plantations, I thought. "How many courses do you have?" I asked, turning to the driver.

"We rotate four," he said.

"How many guns will be out today?"

"There'll be four in your party. This will be the only party out there, so we'll split a course, two working one way from the center and two working the opposite direction."

I turned back to the window to study the plantation layout. The dirt road we were riding on felt like a washboard, its ridges keeping the speed of the truck to less than fifteen miles an hour. I didn't mind since I found it interesting to examine how professionals manage a large body of land.

"We have some chaps you can use over those jeans you're wearing," Johnny said, somewhat with a sneer, or at least that was my impression. "There are a lot of briars and thorns in a quail field and your thighs will take a bloody beating without some protection." His comments pulled me back from my thoughts about how this tabletop flatland differed totally from the undulating land I had walked over at the quail hunts I enjoyed in the past.

"I'm sorry, what did you say?"

"I said we have chaps for your legs. You must not have hunted much quail, because you'd know jeans are not the best pants because of the briars and thorns in the fields."

"That won't be necessary. These are tin cloth jeans, so the briars and thorns won't penetrate them, but thanks anyway,"

I said with a smile even though his condescending attitude and assumption about my lack of experience were irritating.

"Really? That's cool. Where'd you get them?" he asked with genuine curiosity.

"They're made in Washington state by an American company. Go online." I returned to studying the landscape. We rounded a curve, and the settlement came into view.

The plantation belonged to one individual until it passed into corporate hands, a testimony to the cost of running a hunting preserve, just like the cost of operating a private jet, a yacht, or multiple homes. There was a lodge where overnight guests stayed, several outbuildings containing an outdoor kitchen and tables under a shed, a freestanding building with a walk-in freezer and meat locker, and a mechanical shed for maintaining the various equipment. The clubhouse was complete with a menagerie of taxidermy animals ranging from deer heads to beavers to six-foot rattle snakes looking down from the walls. A lounge area was spacious; there were lockers for members and a kitchen for serving food. To the other side of the clubhouse was a barn sheltering two horses and a chicken house with egg-laying shelves and a wire-enclosed yard, protecting the birds from both flying predators and walking ones. Next to the barn, surrounded by a twelve-foot-tall wood-and-wire fence, was a garden plot of about a half-acre. Very little was being grown, with most of the plot abandoned by the caretakers.

They arranged all the structures in a half circle, and the dirt road circled a center live oak tree. The structures were in a grove of stately trees, many likely over a hundred years old. It looked like someone who understood the summer heat in southeast Georgia made the best use of the shade from these majestic sentinels. Johnny pulled his pickup next to a bird buggy. We exited. I took my gun, and he grabbed my gun bag and coat and walked over to the buggy. He put my things on one of the upper seats and held out his hand for my gun, interestingly, placing it with breech open on the driver's seat. I saw Henry, my friend and host, and walked over to shake his hand.

Henry is an accomplished outdoorsman. From an early age, hunting and fishing was a way of life. His family made infrequent but regular trips to Africa for trophy safaris. Not only did he know how to hunt, but he also looked the part of a hunter. His Barbour field jacket had seen many days of sun, rain, dirt, and game blood. It fit like a custom-tailored glove. His pants were the typical quail-hunting pants with a sheath of tough cloth covering the legs up to the crotch. Just like the jacket and the plaid shirt, the pants were no stranger to the fields, stands, and swamps. He had brushed mud from his last hunt off his boots, but clean was not the object of the exercise. His blaze-orange watch cap was the only nod to complying with the state laws for hunting safety.

"Welcome," he said. "We're having some biscuits, butter, molasses, and coffee. Have some."

I walked over to the table, poured a cup of coffee, got a paper plate, opened a biscuit, smeared it with butter, and poured on syrup. Just as I stuffed a large piece of the sweet delight in my mouth, two guys across the table looked up from their plates and stood.

"These are our shooting partners," Henry said.

Swallowing quickly, I said, "Morning," and held out my hand to the nearest guy.

"Fred," he said, shaking hands. Fred had on a blaze-orange-and-green cap with Estes Plantation embroidered on the front, a tan-and-blaze-orange shirt with the Estes Plantation emblem, new quail-hunting pants, and a leather belt with a silver-tinted buckle and an Estes Plantation silver medallion on the belt's side, all obviously just off the rack in the lodge gift shop. His boots were high-top L. L. Bean hunting boots. He looked like a *Gardens & Guns* magazine ad, a fantasy read for young Southern men and women who dreamed about the rich before and after the Civil War. The idea is to take the mystical pre-Civil War plantation life, mix it with working young adults, shake well, and pour out a special person who drinks exotic bourbon whiskey and craft beers with a fruity taste and eats five-course dinners outside under the oak trees, dressed in tailored clothes from England, Scotland, and Italy.

"Just call me Justin," the other hunter said, shaking my hand. While I thought the South's favorite magazine outfitted Fred, Justin Sprague IV was straight out of a Beretta catalogue. I quickly glanced around, looking for the photographer team shooting this hunt for Justin's Facebook page. While Fred had all new duds bought in the lodge, Justin's tailored clothes were not off the lodge rack. His shooting coat was wool, in a hunter-green-and-tan herringbone pattern, with real bone-and-leather buttons. Since this wasn't Scotland, he didn't have on a tie. There was a pair of white cotton gloves hanging out of his left breast pocket like a handkerchief. I thought that was strange but said nothing. His tan shirt tucked into a pair of brown wool pants with ballistic cloth on the thighs, and his pant legs were inside a pair of green Wellington calf-length rubber boots. A gentleman hunter from the bonny hills of Scotland, if there ever was one. While the day was cool and crisp, the southern sun, when it was up high, would prove to Justin that this was not the Highlands.

The white gloves were on my mind, but I didn't want to ask a stupid question, so I held my tongue. "Justin, good morning. These biscuits are wonderful," I responded, taking another bite, still looking at the white gloves. When among a bunch of men, particularly in a manly setting like a group about to go hunting, asking a question that immediately marks the questioner as a dunce or novice is the last thing a guy wants to do, but the gloves were hanging out of his pocket like a kid in the second grade waving his arm so the teacher would pick him to answer the question. I turned my attention back to breakfast so I wouldn't ask the stupid question.

Bo sipped his coffee to wash down a mouthful of sweetness and said, "How much do you fellas know about these pint-sized jet engines we're going to intercept today?" He looked at the four of us to see if anyone would answer.

"Well," Fred began, wiping his mouth and then sticking his hands in his pockets, "since you asked, the genus is *Colinus virginanus*, of which there are five subspecies in North America. The one we're hunting is *virginanus*, commonly called the bobwhite quail. It's found from north Florida over to Texas and up to Minnesota and Michigan. Our hunting the birds isn't a big deal. They'll be dead in two years, anyway. Either the weather gets them or a predator, which could be a raccoon, opossum, weasel, mink, bobcat, Cooper's or sharp-shinned hawk, marsh hawk, horned or barred owl, blue jay, crow, or wild or domesticated turkey. It's believed the ancestor of the bobwhite was living in Kansas over a million years ago, and they found a fossil of the bobwhite in Florida, dating back fifteen-thousand years ago. They fly at speeds of up to forty miles an hour for a short distance."

We all stood in utter silence as Fred finished his brain dump about quail. He obviously liked to know about what he was doing.

Bo broke the silence. "If you shoot as good as you talk, we're going to need some more birds in the fields. Let's get loaded up while those little ones are still sleepy." He went over to the two bird buggies and opened the gun boxes on the back of each. "Mark and Henry, you two will ride out with me. If you'll give me your guns, we'll store them for the ride."

Henry handed him his .410, a gun that had seen many hunts and had been modified with removable chokes.

"Old trusty, eh? You must be serious today," Bo said, obviously knowing the gun and Henry, who just chuckled and walked to the front of the buggy.

I handed Bo my 20-gauge over-and-under.

"I'll be damned," he said, "a B. C. Mikrou gun." He turned it over and over. "They made this one in Japan—one of the good ones. I haven't seen one of these for a while. Skeet and skeet boring. You'd better be quick, or it'll be a long day." He took the gun, closed the breech, and put it in the box.

Shooting is like any other skill sport, such as golf or tennis. Confidence in your own ability counts for most success on any day. That self-confidence is fragile—just ask any sports psychologist, of which there are many today, in this age of wanting to perform to unwarranted expectations. Some participants enjoy shattering that feeling of competency in others when on the playing field. Bo's comments fell into that realm, testing a person's focus on enjoying the hunt by sowing the seeds of self-doubt.

I'd met alpha males like Bo before. I looked at him, smiled, and said, "You're right."

Jerry, the other guide, was preparing the second bird buggy. Bo shut the gun box on our vehicle, walked over to other gun box, and opened it. Fred handed him a Browning 12-gauge over-and-under that looked new.

"Fine gun," Bo said, and put the gun in its slot in the box.

Justin had gotten into the buggy with his gun box. It was canvas, with leather corners and leather belts with brass fittings. "I thought I'd carry mine up here with me," he said to Bo in an authoritarian voice.

"That's a mighty fine case you have there, and I'm sure that's a mighty fine gun in that case, but there are insurance rules that say all guns must be in the buggy's gun box between here and the field, and from the field back here. Now we have two choices, and I'll let you decide: either the gun goes in here or it doesn't go at all. What'll it be? Your choice." He said this brief response in a tone slightly more authoritative than the one Justin had used. The two of them looked at each other, Bo's jaws working over a plug of tobacco. He turned his head and spit.

Finally, the silence broke by Justin undoing the belts on the gun box in his lap. Before taking the gun out of the case, he put on the white gloves. He gently took out a 12-gauge side-by-side shotgun with a straight stock. Not knowing a lot about guns but reading hunting magazines from time to time, I figured the gun was probably worth $25,000 or more. The engraving on the barrel and breech was exquisite, and the wood of the stock was unlike any I'd ever seen. I couldn't tell who the maker was from where I was standing.

Bo reached up and almost snatched the gun from Justin's hands.

"Please—please be careful," Justin said, hopping down from his seat on the buggy. Bo tried not to show his awe at handling such a gun.

"This is a Purdey, isn't it?" Bo said, looking at Justin. "Tell me about it."

"It's a Purdey, made in the 1920s, 12-gauge, thirty-inch barrels, improved and full chokes. The stock is French walnut. Please let me wipe it before you put it in the gun box," Justin said, taking a gun cloth out of his coat pocket.

"Sure," Bo said, handing the gun back to Justin, who took the gun in his gloved hands and began vigorously wiping the metal and wood with the silicone cloth.

"What'd that gun cost?" Bo asked.

"A lot."

"Did it come with all the misses already taken out?"

Everybody laughed, which I guess Bo wanted to happen. It broke the tension and got him off the hook for being aggressive. None of us had ever seen a Purdey, much less shot one. The gun made a statement about Justin's wealth and desire to have the best hunting equipment, but his skill remained to be seen. Using a 12-gauge to hunt quail was a good sign Justin was neither experienced nor a good shot. It's too much gun for the birds.

"All right, let's load up and go get dinner," Bo said. Henry and I got in Bo's buggy, and Justin and Fred sat on the upper seats of Jerry's buggy.

I've been on quail hunts, riding on horses and riding in a wagon with red leather seats, pulled by a matched pair of mules, but never in custom-made buggies like the ones at the Estes Plantation. These were pickup trucks with the roof, doors, and windshield removed. Behind the two front seats, there was a raised area housing four dog boxes with a step up to a bench seat for two passengers. The back of the buggies had a box for four guns. Just below the doors to the dog boxes on each side was a box running the length of the sides that held shells. On the front of each buggy was a wire platform attached to the front frame for the retriever to sit. Leashes with buckles attached to the collar allowed the dog some movement but no chance of falling off or jumping down from the perch. These buggies are an outdoorsman's dream transportation. They oozed manliness and superiority. The excitement of the hunt grew as we pulled away, all of us chattering and laughing. Shortly, the pointers would move rapidly, looking for coveys. The birds would fly, and the guns would bark. The day was perfect, cool with a clear sky, and our confidence was as high as it would be all day.

Bo slowed his lead buggy as we came to the sporting clay field. "Anybody want to do a little clay shooting to get the misses out of your gun?" he inquired.

Henry said no, and I shook my head. In any competitive skill sport, whether you're with friends or strangers, there's a chance of flubbing the shot or stroke, so it's a time of acute anxiety for most of us. Having that moment when one's skill is on display with everyone standing around watching, like the first drive on the first hole of a golf course, was not for any of us. When the first covey rises in the field, when just your shooting partner and your guide will see how badly you shoot, is tough enough. Bo put the buggy in gear and proceeded to the quail field.

Without a windshield, even at ten miles per hour, the cold air enveloped us, penetrated all the thin layers of clothing and coats, reached our bodies, and let us know without a doubt that winter was on the way. I cursed at myself for not having enough sense to put on my field coat. I looked around and realized I was the only dumbass without a jacket on. Coming back, when the sun would be high, the lack of a windshield would be a challenge for another reason. Riding through the swamp, the woods, and the open fields is an experience that stirs the soul. Being close to nature, and soon actively interacting with it, made me realize how much being an urban dweller takes away from the human connection with the natural world.

We arrived at an intersection of one road going north and south and another going east and west. Bo and Jerry pulled to a stop. The dogs started howling and moving around in their boxes, and we all piled out.

"Here we are, gentlemen. Your opponent awaits you. If you don't want to go to bed hungry, I suggest you don't miss." Bo unleashed the retriever. "This here is Nellie. She's a purebred lab with a nose that won't quit and a mouth as tender as a baby's butt. You put a bird down and she'll find it and bring it to me without a tooth mark on it, even if it's still wiggling."

Nellie ran around, marking a spot every few seconds and looking like she was remembering she had been here before. Bo walked to the side of the buggy, opened one box door at a time, and pulled out two pointers, helping them jump to the ground. All the time, the dogs howled their heads off. On the ground, they joined Nellie, moving at full speed, their noses to the ground. They stopped momentarily to pee, and then their thick paws sounded like distant rumbling thunder as they stomped around.

"The one with faint tan spots is Sugar, and the other is Sandy. I trained both pointers and Nellie myself, so they know what they're doing." Bo went around to the back of the buggy and opened the gun box. "Don't shoot my dogs," Bo said, looking me in the eye as he handed me my gun, breech open. He handed Henry his gun. "There're shells in those side boxes. Help yourself." He nodded.

I opened the shell box and took out two boxes of 20-gauge, emptying them into the left bellows pocket of my vest. Henry dug out a box of .410 and dumped it into his right coat pocket.

"All right, fellas, let's see what the ladies can find," Bo said as he gave two short blasts on a whistle. The pointers stopped their random wandering and looked back at Bo. His arm went up and then straight out in front of him. The two dogs came running and began working the area about ten to fifteen yards in front of Bo. I took up a position to his right while Henry moved to Bo's left. Henry and I had our shotguns' breeches open, resting on our right shoulders, holding onto the stock at its base with our right hands.

What looked like smooth ground covered in wiregrass and thickets of briars was anything but. At some point this vast field, perhaps two-hundred acres, had been a planted pine forest. Over the years the owners thinned trees, burned the debris, and harrowed the ground. It was these harrowed rows that made today's walk challenging, but it really didn't matter. The hunt was on. The excitement and adrenaline were pumping. We were seconds away from the first point, the first covey rise, and the first opportunity to shoot. Sugar was the first to point, and Sandy quickly honored the point.

"All right, fellas," Bo whispered, "remember, you've got twelve o'clock high to three." He nodded in my direction. "Henry, you've got twelve o'clock to nine. I'm going to move and then step past Sugar and beat the grass with my stick. Be ready."

Henry and I walked slowly with Bo, our shotguns loaded with two #7 shells and at the ready, waiting to be pivoted up to our shoulders when the birds flushed. It's hard to say if a quail hunter sees the birds first or hears them first. The roar of the feathers is loud, persistent, and shocking no matter how many times a hunter has heard it. Some novice hunters forget to shoot the first time they hear a covey rise, it's so spectacular. The three of us didn't get to Sugar before the sixteen birds made their escape. Instinctively, I focused on two birds moving from twelve o'clock to two and let go with both barrels. One bird dropped, gliding to the ground, which meant I wounded it. The other bird flew a few more yards and dove for the tall grass. Henry had let go his two barrels and got a bird as well.

Bo began hollering, "Dead, dead, here, Nellie, dead, dead!" repeatedly. Nellie found Henry's bird first and brought it to Bo. A clean kill. "Dead, dead, Nellie, dead, dead!" Bo repeated and pointed in the direction my bird had fallen. Nellie took off and within a minute had found my bird, barely alive. She brought it back to Bo, who casually took the bird by the head and gave it a twirl, snapping its neck. "Good shooting, fellas. It's obvious you've both done this a few times." He mostly aimed his comments at me, since he had hunted with Henry for years.

I felt relieved, not embarrassed. The first flush was over, and I got my bird. The two pointers were back working the grass. There was no time to gloat. Our guns were back over our shoulders, breeches open, as we regrouped and followed the dogs and Bo. Not only were we looking for a covey, but also the remnants of the covey we'd just shot. These singles are just as challenging as full coveys. A single or pair of birds can try running on the ground, get up low and stay low. This is when an inexperienced gunner may lose discipline, aim low, and shoot a dog. Sugar pointed again, and again Sandy honored the point.

"This here is a single or a handful because this is where the first covey put down," Bo said.

I reached into my vest, put two shells between my fingers, shifted my gun off my shoulder, placed the shells in the breech, and snapped it shut. The three of us moved in and passed Sugar and Sandy before two birds rose and flew low and to the ten o'clock position. Henry's gun barked and one bird was down.

As we meandered around the ground we were hunting, Bo asked, "You fellas married?"

Henry answered no, and I said yes.

"Me and my wife," Bo continued, "have our twenty-fifth wedding anniversary coming up. We were going to go on a cruise, but they have diagnosed my wife with fibro-something or another, which requires some medicine our insurance doesn't cover. Can you believe people have to pay four-hundred dollars a month for some little pills? That's what we were going to have to pay for the three-day cruise to the Bahamas. She hardly ever got sick before now. It just doesn't seem right—you pay three hundred a month for insurance, and it isn't worth squat. Just not right. But you know, the Lord will provide. We read the Bible and pray every night that she'll get well and that we'll not need that medicine. Her biggest joy is our new grandbaby, a girl our son and his wife just had. Both the parents need to work to make ends meet, so Gloria, that's my wife, has been keeping the little one. She says she loves it, but I figure that's why she's gotten sick, and we won't be able to go on the cruise."

"That's a shame," I said, shaking my head and hoping the dog would point soon to stop the conversation. Trying to be invisible, Henry just watched the dogs.

"You know, God always provides. I know my wife deserves to have a nice twenty-fifth anniversary and God will answer our prayers. We have a Prayer Warrior Room at our church. Me and some of Gloria's friends go in that room before services on Sunday and before Bible study Wednesday evenings, and we pray hard, real hard, so she'll get better and we'll find the extra money." Bo rambled on in between covey rises and while waiting for Nellie to bring back the quail.

The two hours we spent covering our designated territory went by fast. Henry bagged more birds than I did. My success hovered around 50 percent. His was closer to 80 percent. It didn't matter to me at all. The hunt was everything I wanted it to be. With all our trekking, following the flights of the birds, we finished close to the buggies two hours after we began.

"How'd you fellas do?" Bo asked Justin and Fred, while looking at Jerry.

"They did really good," Jerry responded, winking at Bo with a grin on his face.

Bo began putting Sugar and Sandy back in their boxes. They were quiet, proud of their work, and tired. Howls were going up from the two fresh dogs Bo helped down from their boxes. He said to Fred and Justin, "All right, you gentlemen have the pleasure of hunting with me; Nellie, the black retriever over there; Cracker, the pointer with the small spots; and Peppy, the smaller pointer, who is young and anxious. Grab some shells and we'll get started."

Jerry turned to Henry and me, saying, "Okay, gentlemen, we'll be working with Blue over there, the retriever; Rip, the larger of the two pointers; and Queenie, the female. She got her name from being downright angry when she points birds and the shooters miss." He lowered his voice and said with a grin, "It's a damn good thing she wasn't working the first course. She'd be livid about now."

Jerry preferred to use a leather strap rather than a stick to beat the wiregrass and briars, trying to scare a covey into flushing. It wasn't long before the dogs had found the first covey. The hunting went about the same as the first tour, with Henry continuing to show his mastery of his .410 and the field. Jerry was mostly quiet, giving compliments where they were due and making excuses for us, mainly me, when necessary.

About an hour into the hunt, Jerry asked nobody in particular, "Do you have any children?"

"Yes, I have two, but they're grown and parents of their own," I said. After uttering these words, I realized Jerry knew Henry well, since he was a member of Estes, so he would know Henry was single and didn't have any children.

"Then you have grandchildren. What age are they?"

"The girl is eleven, and the boy is nine."

"I have one, a little girl aged eight. She's a special needs child, but she can function pretty well. We have her in public school, where they have classes and teachers who know how to handle children with developmental difficulties."

Jerry's carefully worded explanation impressed me.

"The challenge for Amy, that's my daughter, and her mother is my wife's unwillingness to allow Amy to think that she can't do anything any other child can do. Earline, that's my wife, has Amy in special tutoring sessions after school. It costs me two-hundred dollars a month. That's a lot of money for us cause Earline can't work. She volunteers at the school where Amy attends just so she can be there if Amy loses control."

I groped for a response and finally said, "Will your daughter grow out of this situation?"

"They tell us maybe. We pray each night with Amy, asking God to help her and teach her the right way to be." As soon as Jerry said the words, Queenie pointed at a covey.

I whipped my gun off my shoulder while reaching into my vest pocket for two shells. Loading and snapping the gun closed, I stepped forward, in line with Jerry and Henry. As the roar began, I focused on my quadrant and brought down a bird at the outer limits for a 20-gauge.

I was proud of my shot until I heard Jerry shout, "A twofer! Man, you got a twofer!" I thought he was talking to me until I saw him high-five Henry. A twofer in quail hunting is like a hole-in-one in golf. It takes skill and luck. Those who have never had one say it's pure luck. Those who have understood the skill necessary to realize instantly, without conscious thought, that two birds are crossing paths and will be close to each other for a fleeting millisecond. One shot and two birds. The thrill can make your entire year. It didn't surprise me that Henry got one. I was both pleased for him and envious of his skill. Jerry was excited. His gunner had gotten a twofer. He'd have reflected glory as the guide.

Our hunting from then on was upbeat and fast-paced. Jerry seemed to have forgotten his travails with his daughter. Shortly after the sun was directly overhead, Bo hollered and told everybody the hunt was over. We had a good morning. Our legs realized the lengths we had walked and stood for four hours. Jerry called the dogs back to the buggy. Blue and Rip came running, but Queenie was nowhere to be seen.

Bo took Justin's and Fred's guns and put them in the gun box. He came over to us, opened the other gun box, and said, "What was all that ruckus about, Henry? Are you saving the plantation money on shells?"

Henry blushed and responded, "You know quail, Bo. They do crazy things like trying to fly into shot patterns." Jerry was blowing on his whistle and finally pulled out what looked like an old-fashioned cell phone from the 1990s, big and bulky with a small screen.

"Queenie is in the back of the field, Bo. We'll go get her while y'all head back for lunch."

"How do you know where she is?" I asked.

"This little gadget," Jerry said, holding up the old phone item. "This is a GPS instrument. All the dogs have a GPS positioner on their collar, along with an attention-getter. All we do is follow the signal on this device and we'll go right to her. If she's on point, she'll stay that way all day long. So let's go see if you have one more chance to get a twofer like Henry."

The three of us piled into the second buggy, and Jerry, with the GPS locator in his hand held next to the steering wheel, drove across the field. Sure enough, Queenie was on point.

"Grab your guns from the box, fellas, and let's have one more chance at dinner."

We lined up as we had all morning, and the three of us moved slowly by Queenie. One bird flew straight out at twelve o'clock. Neither of us fired. There's a strange thing about hunting, particularly quail hunting. The activity is physical: the walking, carrying a six-pound gun for four hours, the tension of the covey rise. When it's over, the stamina seems to slip away at the same time. We just stood there as Jerry put Queenie in her box.

When we arrived back at the lodge, Jerry pulled the buggy next to Bo's.

"I'm going to help Bo clean the birds. You fellas help yourselves to lunch. Save room for the cobbler—Johnny makes the best in this part of the state," Jerry said as he picked up the cooler containing our successes for the morning.

Fred and Justin were already sitting at the table. Fried chicken, mashed potatoes, and green beans cooked with ham hocks covered Fred's plate, and a side plate of corn bread sat alongside the molasses bottle. Justin was munching on a chicken leg, his plate heaped with green beans and cornbread, no mashed potatoes. The staff had set places for Henry and me. In the middle of the table, between the two seats on each side, was a small, shallow bucket. I almost took it as a centerpiece. Henry and I went and fixed our plates and got our sweet tea. Sometimes I think the tea is the best part of the meal on these hunts, particularly if it's ice cold. I examined the cobbler—it looked like peach—and knew I didn't want to fill up on chicken and green beans.

"Did you enjoy the hunt?" Henry said to no one in particular.

"It was okay," Fred said. Justin was quiet.

"How'd the Purdey shoot, Justin? This your first time in the field with it?" Henry continued the twenty-questions game, attempting to engage the two across the table in conversation.

"It did fine," Justin said, putting down the cleaned chicken bone and wiping his mouth and hands on the paper towel in his lap. He offered no further information. The table fell silent.

"What's the bucket for?" I asked Henry, realizing what it was for but understanding that the two across the table wouldn't even notice it.

"That's where we put the gratuity for the guides."

"Gratuity? What do you mean, gratuity? This morning cost us five-hundred bucks. At the hotel they just add the gratuity onto the bill. I thought the five-hundred included the gratuity. It had to at that price." Fred was talking so fast with a mouthful of chicken we almost couldn't understand him.

"What's customary?" Justin inquired.

"The regular amount is forty dollars per gun, but if you feel they went above and beyond, perhaps fifty dollars per gun."

"And if they weren't up to snuff?" Justin said, a seriousness in his voice and on his face.

"Anything you feel is appropriate," Henry said, holding Justin's gaze.

Justin pulled out his wallet and put thirty dollars in the bucket.

Fred, reaching for his wallet, said "I've certainly had better guides." He opened his wallet and, without realizing it, exposed the fact that he had only a twenty-dollar bill in it. Taking the twenty out, he tossed it in the bucket and went back to eating his food faster than he did before the anteing up. He stopped with a mouthful, got up, went over to the serving table, put two heaping spoons of cobbler in a Styrofoam bowl, and brought it back to his place. He then resumed his speed-eating.

Henry pulled a fifty-dollar bill from his wallet and put it in the bucket. I pulled three twenties from my wallet, put them in the bucket, and pulled out the ten Justin had tossed in, holding it carefully so everyone could see it was a ten and not a twenty.

We ate in silence, each of us measuring the importance and impact of the gratuity conversation. A few minutes went by, with Justin checking his cell phone every minute, before Bo and Jerry reappeared with four small soft-sided coolers stenciled with Estes Plantation and a drawing of a covey rise and hunter on the side.

"Here's dinner, fellas. There are cold packs in these coolers, so you have about an hour and a half before you've got to get these birds in the refrig'. We enjoyed having you. Come back soon." Bo and Jerry put their cooler next to each of us, smiled, and went to fix their lunch plates. They sat in the covered kitchen with Johnny.

The Diviner

"YOU DON'T REALLY BELIEVE it, do you?" I said, reaching for my wine glass.

"Of course not. There's no logic. It's just hocus-pocus BS. Still . . .," she responded with her arms tightly crossed over her chest.

"Still, what? Why are you acting the way you are? You do believe it. I can't believe you." I sat back in my chair with an incredulous look on my face.

I looked across the table at her. Her demeanor and responses were not the typical left-brain interactions I'd grown used to seeing and hearing. Usually, she analyzed and dissected every minute detail of any idea, plan, or proposed outing so much that the mystery and fun were peeled back layer by layer, almost to the point of making a person say, "Why bother?"

"Don't be an ass. I don't believe it, but there are some weird coincidences."

* * *

We woke to a bright blue, late May sky with the joint desire to get out of our small apartment, go urban hiking, and have a great lunch. Then dinner could be light, and we could do more serious hiking when the sun went down and the temperature dropped.

"Any suggestions for where we can have a celebratory lunch in honor of your promotion?" I asked.

"I don't know. It's got to be a place with great food where we can be comfortable in our hiking gear."

"When are they going to announce you're the new executive VP in charge of all R&D?"

"Two weeks," she grunted, pulling on her boots. "That's why that stack of binders is over there. I'm on assignment until Wednesday. It'll give me cover for being gone as I plod through the records to get a broad overview of the lab. Tomorrow through Tuesday is the set study period. I'm ready. Three days of focused reading and analyzing. Nothing to distract me. Piece of cake."

"Well, Ms. EVP, where's lunch?" I asked again, lacing my second boot.

After thirty minutes of analyzing every single alternative, consulting the two-year-old Zagat, and calling numerous restaurants listed in the book to see if they were still open, she closed the Zagat, flipped it onto the glass coffee table, and announced we were going to walk across the park to Bar

Boulud for rainbow trout. There's nothing better in New York City for working up an appetite than a stroll through Central Park. Not only does it burn calories to make room for the new ones, but it lifts your spirits as you watch all the children, dogs, squirrels, birds, and people doing what they want to do with the enthusiasm of toddlers before society regimented them into its approved behavioral structure.

We entered the park at Seventy-Ninth and Fifth, making our first directional decision a few feet into the park. "Which way?" I asked. I learned a long time ago to play follow the leader with the left-brain part of our relationship.

"This way," she said, nodding her head to the south. We started around Cherry Hill. The area was bristling with nannies and parents, their fleet of strollers, and toddlers running around. Get 'em tired—that's the first task of any parent or nanny in the outdoors. As we approached the first bridge over one of the many paths, I noticed an old man sitting on a campstool in front of a folding table. A black cloth covered the top. In front of the table, opposite the old man, was another campstool. My eyes went back to the old man, who seemed to be playing solitaire, turning the cards over and putting them in some order. He was absorbed in what he was doing, not paying attention to anyone else walking by. On the edge of the table was a small, hand-lettered, framed sign: Fortunes Told, $10.

"Look! Have you ever seen that here before? Let's see what's going on," she said, grabbing my hand and pulling me along. As we got closer, I noticed the bandana covering his head, the thick-framed glasses, and the billowy white shirt and frayed suede vest that looked as old as the man himself. What was unusual was the gold and diamond Rolex on his right wrist.

"Hi! How does this work?" she queried the old man. He didn't answer her, just pointed to the seat and the sign.

"Do you have a ten?" she said, looking at me and holding out her hand.

"You're not serious about getting your fortune told, are you?"

"Why not? With what happened yesterday, I'd like to see what he says." I reached into my jacket pocket, extracted my wallet, and gave her a ten. I stood off to the side, watching as she sat down and put the money on the table. The old man reached over and took it with his right hand, removed the sign from the table with his left, and then quickly placed the deck of cards in front of her.

"Take ten deep breaths to clear your mind. Shuffle the cards three times, and while shuffling, ask your question about the future," he said in a heavy Brooklyn accent. He placed both of his hands flat on the table in front of him.

She picked up the well-worn cards, which seemed as pliable as tissue paper. I wondered how much those cards had earned the old man. She sat with her forearms on the table, holding the cards in her hands, breathing deeply with her eyes closed, and counting out loud with each breath. At ten, she opened her eyes and began shuffling. She started with the best shuffle, dividing the cards in two and merging the ends into each other. She did this twice, watching the old man as he stared intently at her.

Then she started sending the cards from one hand to the other as she said, "What will the next phase of my life be like?" She cut her eyes away from the old man to me and winked with her left eye, smiling.

The old man reached for the cards with his right hand, again flashing the huge Rolex. He placed the deck slightly to the side and began dealing the cards, one by one with his right hand, placing them face up. The first card went into the center between the two of them. The second card he placed over the first card, but horizontally instead of vertically. The third card went on the table between the first two cards and where she was sitting. The fourth card went to his right of the first two, which was her left. The fifth card went closer to the old man, on the table between him and the first two cards. The sixth card went alongside the first two on his left, her right, forming a cross. The next four cards were placed in a line to his right and her left, starting on his side of the table, with the last card closest to her. He stopped and removed the rest of the deck from the table. Why place the cards in this pattern, I wondered? I realized the cards were not regular cards in a 52-card deck. The pictures on these cards were brightly colored, intricately drawn, and had a roman numeral and name on them. I felt the excitement of what was to come. She shifted her position on the campstool. I thought about how uncomfortable it must have been to sit on that small circle. I looked at my watch. This reading needed to progress, or we would miss our reservation. On Saturdays, Bar Boulud's maître d' was brutal about giving tardy patrons' tables away since they always had people standing in line. The old man continued to stare at her. He hadn't taken his eyes off of her since she sat down. I wondered if he was staring at her eyes or her ample breasts, visible to some extent in the scoop-necked blouse.

Again, using his right hand while his left was sitting in his lap, he began identifying the cards in the sequence he'd laid them down. Every time he touched a card, he indicated what it represented. "The first card is your present position, and it is the Star." He fingered the second card: "This card represents immediate influences in your life, and it is the Tower." He reached up to touch the third card, saying softly, "This card represents your goal or destiny, and it is the Chariot." I noticed a flinch in his facial features, which he quickly replaced with the stony countenance he had shown since we arrived. Time evaporated. Curiosity transported both of us to a place where nothing mattered except the next card even though we had no idea what the cards were saying. He caressed the fourth card, again with his right hand, which I finally realized was his nondominant hand. Why? Was there significance in using this hand rather than his dominant hand? I'll ask him when he's finished, I thought.

He spoke about the fourth card, whispering, "This card represents the distant past foundation, and it is the Ace of

Wands." He moved to the fifth card, touching it. "This card represents recent past events, and it is the Empress." A fleeting smile crossed his face.

I looked at her and she seemed to perk up, shifting on the stool once more.

He pointed to and then fingered the sixth card. "This card represents future influences, and it is Justice." We seemed to be on a wave of positive vibes. He reached for the seventh card, saying as he touched it, "This card represents the querent"—that's her, I thought—"and is the Death card."

Both of us let out an audible gasp.

He picked up his pace, fingering the eighth and ninth cards in rapid succession. "The eighth card represents environmental factors and is the Queen of Wands, while the ninth card represents inner emotions and is the Knight of Wands." He hesitated. There was only one card left, but the seventh card overshadowed the past cards: our urgency to understand its meaning was rising steadily. He reached for the tenth card, titled the Lovers, and said, "this card represents the final results."

Confusion ricocheted through my mind. Were the cards positive or negative? What did the Death card mean, particularly since it represented her, the querent? What was I doing, giving credence to this fortune-telling? What was she thinking? The fun, serene look that had been her demeanor before the seventh card was gone. She was a left-brain, so there wasn't panic in her face, just annoyance and irritation. Both of us waited for the diviner to begin interpreting the cards.

The old man swept the cards into a pile with his right hand, and, without preamble, said, "You are currently in a good place in your life, both personally and professionally. You have an opportunity to achieve one of your life goals; however, to achieve it, you will have to break from all of the features of your current life that give you happiness and safety. Your future journey to higher success will be difficult since you will be required to detach yourself from the reality that surrounds you and focus all your physical and mental abilities on your goal. There is risk, and the cost to your personal life may be higher than you want to pay. Your whole life since childhood has prepared you for this opportunity, in particular the discipline you have nurtured and strengthened in the last five years. There is a challenge, however, to achieving your goal. The person you are may die in this life quest you have in front of you. You will not know if this demise will happen until you are so far into the garden of intellectual growth needed to achieve your goal that the path of return will be lost to you. Your inner emotions are in a good place, and you believe you are ready for the journey, but that is because you can't fully comprehend the risks and challenges ahead. Beware of both professional and personal life obstacles. If you are willing to undertake the journey, if you have the fortitude to accept the necessary changes in your life, the end result will be everything you anticipate, with the costs potentially greater than you expect."

"Help me understand what you're saying," she pleaded. I could tell she was agitated. I looked at my watch. Damn. Our reservation was at risk. We were already halfway through the grace period. I had to call them. I pulled out my phone and turned my back to the table.

As the phone was ringing, I heard the old man say, "I've told you all that the cards say." He gathered the cards, put them back into a black silk pouch, and deposited the pouch in a pocket of his vest. He then put both hands on the table. He ignored her and me. It was obvious the engagement was over. I touched her elbow, indicating she should stand.

She stood but said, "I don't understand everything. You need to clarify what you said. Please explain the risks you talk about. Tell me how to avoid the obstacles, how to handle them. Please." I was trying to move us along, but she wouldn't budge.

"The cards have spoken. There is no more to say." He looked away.

"Please, we have to go. I called and they'll only hold our reservation for ten more minutes."

We started walking away, but she looked back at the old man. He was sitting calmly at the table, having put the fortune telling sign back in its place.

"We have to go back and make him clarify what he said." She hesitated.

"Look, we have to get to the restaurant. Besides, he told you there's nothing more to be said. You can't hold a gun to his head."

"But it's not fair. He said things that need clarifying. He has to be fair and explain what he means."

"He'll only repeat that the cards said everything. Just calm down. We'll discuss this in a rational manner at the restaurant."

"How can you even think about eating after what just happened?"

"Primarily because I'm hungry and their trout is out of this world."

* * *

"Weird? That's a strange word coming from you. I always thought logic was the basis of your life and everything you believed. Hmm, I guess getting your fortune told by an old guy in Central Park isn't terribly logical either," I said when we had ordered and were sipping our wine.

"I'm a scientist. Seeing that guy just sitting there in the park just made it, I don't know, spontaneous and exciting. I guess I was looking for affirmation of what was happening."

"Well, you got it, so to speak. Just—how do you say it—not exactly the way your fantasy envisioned it. Maybe that's good in and of itself."

"How do you mean?"

"The cards—"

"You mean the diviner."

"The cards—"

"Stop with the cards. You sound like that little guy on that TV show: 'De plane! De plane!' Besides, he didn't even look like one of those people."

"What people?"

"You know: those people, like gypsies. They're usually on the third floor of a ratty building in some poor neighborhood where people believe all that crap," she snapped.

"The old man said the cards told the story and he just interpreted it, so don't get hostile with me."

"I'm not hostile, just uneasy. What if what he says is true? Will I lose you? Will I lose my friends? What'll happen? Is it too much to ask for clarification? Christ, it only seems fair to have a greater understanding of what to expect."

"Hey, wait a minute. You *know* nobody knows the future, so why the agitation over clarity? Crystal balls are foggy."

"Yeah, but how did he know I was considering the biggest promotion of my life?"

"He didn't know. The cards knew."

"God almighty, there you go again with the cards. Okay, smartass, how did the cards know?"

"You told them."

"I didn't say a word. Not one word. You know that. You were standing right there."

"Not out loud. But remember how he told you to clear your mind before picking up the cards? When you were shuffling the cards, you were told to think about your question and then to announce your question to the diviner and the cards. Your hands and your subconscious told the cards."

"What have you been smoking?" she retorted angrily.

"Don't get angry with me. Even your question gave the diviner and the cards a clue. 'What will the next phase of my life be like?' I thought the reading was, well, overall positive."

The waiter brought our trout almandine. My mouth started watering. I took a bite of my fish with some broccoli and wild rice. "God, this is as great as ever. You need to eat yours before it gets cold."

"Why? According to this—what did you call him—diviner, I'm going to be dead soon." She picked at her fish with her fork.

"Neither he nor the cards said that."

"Yes, they did."

"He and the cards said that part of your life up to now will die as you move into this next phase of your life."

"He might not have wanted to tell me the truth—the cards' truth—just to humor me, expecting me to pay him another ten dollars. That's it. I should have offered him another ten bucks."

"It doesn't work that way. The cards tell the story. You're in a good place. You have a solid foundation. You're a vivacious, smart, and exciting person. Oh yeah, and good looking also. I noticed he never took his eyes off your tits during the reading."

"His eyes were looking directly into my eyes. You're the only guy who can't keep his eyes above a woman's neck."

"That's not true. Don't get hostile with me just because you're upset about the reading."

"I'm not hostile, just stating facts. What do you think he means by 'costs' of achieving my goal? He doesn't even know what the goal is, so how can he talk about the costs associated with the goal?"

"Now you're thinking like a scientist. Any goal anyone strives for has costs associated with it. Costs in terms of time, maybe money, for sure a narrowing of interests, which may cost friendships since you'll be higher in your profession or social status or even become the boss of some of your friends. You'll become responsible for the inputs and outputs of the lab. You'll be rating the performance of your former colleagues. That's always dicey. You can't tell me, or at least I hope you can't, that you haven't thought about these issues."

"Frankly, I haven't given much thought to just how far I stretch to reach the brass ring, so to speak. My friendships at the lab, and for that matter, outside the lab, are important to me. You're important to me." She looked at me with wide, fearful eyes and a trembling chin. "What am I supposed to do?"

"First, finish your trout and your wine. Second, think through the issues raised by the cards and regain your self-confidence."

"Let's walk back though the park and see if he's still there. I can pay another ten dollars and ask a different question."

"Whatever." I signaled for the check.

The Mentor

H E SAT IN THE same restaurant, at the same table, and in the same chair where he had enjoyed lunch every day of the week for the last thirty-five years whenever he was in the city, which was more often now. The restaurant had a narrow front room, with single tables along the left wall and a walkway on the right, opening into a more traditional restaurant room with five rows containing four tables each. A partial wall hid the last single table in the front from the main dining room, that table always reserved for the professor to give him privacy from other patrons. In addition, when the professor was there, no one unknown to the professor or to Carmine lunched at the table immediately behind the wall separating him from the main dining room.

On the back wall of the primary room was a six-foot-by-eight-foot black-and-white photograph of an ancient village in

Macedonia. The other walls held smaller photos from various Macedonian villages, the inhabitants wearing traditional peasant work clothes: patched heavy shirts; ill-fitting pants cinched tight by a too-big belt or section of rope; rough, scuffed boots, only partly tied; and a look of fierce pride and confidence on their faces. Carmine, the host and principal server, stood at his station across the narrow room from the professor's table.

Three books, one in English, one in Russian, and one in French, sat on the table by the professor's left hand. Special books, he found them in a sidewalk bookstall when he was a young man studying in Paris. He considered that day one of the most important in his life. From that point, he knew what his future would be like, where he would spend the rest of his life, and what he would be doing. The books were old then, all three printed in the 1820s, but the leather bindings showed the care and reverence their former owner, or owners, had for the writers and words. They were the first books he purposefully bought as an adult. Around these three books, a four-thousand-book library of knowledge and wisdom grew over the years. When buying books, he sought the first printing, the only version he deemed worthy of his library, not because it was the first edition, like so many book collectors who cherished a book for itself rather than what it said, but because he always wanted to be close to the author's first true words and thoughts, not later revisions that may reflect political correctness or the demands of a higher authority.

He moved his right hand to the lower patch pocket of his Harris wool tweed sports coat, his favorite for the chilly late-fall weather he enjoyed. He fished out a packet of powder and placed it on the table next to his iPhone 6. His fingers searched for the phone while he continued looking at the front door. He momentarily shifted his gaze downward: 12:50 p.m.—ten minutes, if Saba's on time. His instincts became more acute as the time drew near. He smiled, congratulating himself on having Angelina, the beautiful Angelina, sanitize the phone, one last favor from the eternally grateful woman he saved many years ago. He looked over at Carmine and nodded. Carmine brought over a glass of red wine, a basket of bread, and a glass of water. Placing each in its correct position on the table, having to shift the books slightly, Carmine poured some olive oil in a saucer.

"Our best chianti, Professor, from deep in the cellar. I know you will like it."

"Thank you, Carmine. If you selected it, I'm sure I will. How's the family?"

"The wife is fine. The bambinos are growing like weeds, with tongues like prickly pears. Will you be having the usual today?"

"Little ones no longer respect their elders. I've found a good tap on the rump does wonders for opening their ears and shutting their mouths. Yes, I will."

"Are you expecting a guest?"

"Yes, my young friend Sabastian. Ask him immediately what he wants for lunch. It's important I'm walking out of the restaurant precisely at 1:55 p.m. Can you make this happen, my friend?"

"Of course, Professor."

Keeping his right hand on the table, covering the packet of white powder, the professor reached into his right inner coat pocket with his left hand, pulling out a thick envelope and handing it to Carmine. "Put this somewhere safe until you get home, Carmine. Don't open it or look at it. No one is to know you have it." Carmine realized the envelope was too thick to fit in his jeans pocket, so he unbuttoned the shirt button at his waist and slid the envelope into his shirt, just above his belt line.

"Yes, Professor. Is everything all right? Do you need assistance?"

Rodman waved his left hand in dismissal. "No, my friend. There's nothing you can do. Make sure your bambinos grow up and take good care of you and Isabella." Carmine turned and went to his station.

The professor punched the iPhone again: 1:00 p.m. Saba is late, again, just as he knew Saba would be. The professor unfolded the wax paper surrounding the powder, poured the powder into his wineglass, and stirred the wine with his fork. He replaced the fork on the white tablecloth and watched as a spot of red wine from the fork's tines spreads outward, just as knowledge and influence spread when handled correctly. He lifted the glass and drank it all, silently toasting his life.

Seconds later a man in his thirties burst through the restaurant's door, shedding his outer coat, holding it out for

Carmine to take, and sat at the professor's table. "I'm sorry I'm late. A student stayed after class to arrange for a special testing session."

"Saba, you're always late, so why say you're sorry? No jacket? Your generation doesn't understand the subtle ways to make the students respect you. They dress like peasants. You, the teacher, should dress like an authority, always wearing a jacket in class. The students, they are your lifeblood. Take care of them, but demand respect." Carmine appeared at the table with a menu in his hand.

"Professor Rodman is having his usual. What will you be having, Mr. Sabastian?"

"I'll have what he's having, but no wine, just water," Sabastian replied.

"Very good, sir," Carmine said.

"What are you reading?" Sabastian said, canting his head toward the books.

"They're for you. These are the three books I used to start my library. They should be the cornerstone of your library. How many books do you have now?"

"Maybe twenty-five or thirty. Julia won't let me have too many. The apartment is too small, she said, so I can only keep them in my school office, which is the size of a closet."

"Saba, when are you going to be the man of the house? Go find a place big enough for your family with a special room for you. Stretch, reach higher than you can afford, you won't regret it. The debt will keep you focused on your career and you'll have your library with floor-to-ceiling bookshelves for your book collection. This is important for you and your career. Trust me about this."

"Thanks for these." Sabastian reached over and shifted the books to his side of the table. He picked up the top volume and turned it in his hands. "Magnificent. They don't make books like these anymore."

"No, and they don't put words in books like they used to. What's inside is more important than the binding. Why you, Saba?" Rodman asked in a low voice, turning to look directly at his protégé.

Sabastian didn't look up from the book in his hand and responded, "I don't know. I guess they feel we're close enough for you to care about me and my family's welfare."

"What do you mean?" Rodman asked. The professor felt the powder's effect. His lips were tingling and hot, causing him to wet them constantly with his tongue.

Sabastian put the book down and turned to look at Rodman. "They told me they can't give me any more assignments unless I get the contact list and the cash to ensure a safe extraction."

"Can't or won't?"

"Does it matter? Without the money from the assignments, Professor, you know I can't live the life I do, much less get a proper apartment. Their money pays for the children's St. William's tuition and Julia's clothes. God, the clothes she says she needs to be dressed properly as a professor's wife."

"They don't have a right to blackmail you."

"Right? Jesus Christ, you know they don't need a right. They decide what's right or wrong. You know they control the situation. You must understand; I must do what they request—demand. As the godfather of my little Saba and Charlotte, you can't want them to go to a public school or move to a dangerous neighborhood. You must understand my dilemma."

"I promised you, and I will not let you down. I'll give you the information to get the list of names, the security codes, and everything else."

"What about the money? You told me there were more than a million euros you skimmed from them. What about the money?" Sabastian asked anxiously, looking with pleading eyes at Rodman, who was rubbing his left arm with his right hand. The itching was accelerating. He knew it was the powder. The Haitian was specific about how he could gauge the minutes he had left as the powder coursed through his body. He punched his iPhone: 1:20. He was on schedule.

"The money is there, Saba, at least most of it. Some is ensuring a good friend will have what he needs for his bambinos. Do you remember when I told you about my time in Athens, as a young professor like you? Have you been to **Skopje,** Saba?"

"No, I haven't, and you've told me that story—many times, as a matter of fact." Sabastian drank his water and held up his glass for Carmine to bring more. The professor shook his head.

"Well then, I won't bore you with the story again. That's the trouble with history professors, particularly ones who enjoy studying **society** in **general**. We repeat ourselves. Tell me, when was your last assignment and where was it?"

"You know I can't do that. Please, Professor, give me the information. You promised. Once I have it, I'll have power over them. I'll be able to negotiate with them for assignments and a decent stipend."

"Saba, my dear Saba, do you really think you'll have power over them? That you can negotiate with them? You're more foolish than I thought. They respected me because they knew I didn't need them. They knew I did what they directed me to and, on my own, set up a network of younger, more ambitious nationalist activists who have the intense drive and ambition to make their countries a place for good people to prosper. Your so-called friends helped my secret network and received better intelligence than anyone else in that part of Europe. I'm now **seventy-eight** years old and you are **half that**, and that's what's important."

"I'm not thirty-nine, I'm thirty-seven."

"**Half my age is important**, Saba. Don't quibble over meaningless amounts."

"Professor, your contacts can become my contacts. I can go on helping them achieve their goals. Please let me have the list."

"Saba, you can't help them. Everyone on the list has risen to a position of power and influence in their country. No one other than me knows who they are, and they trust me not to reveal their identity."

"Rodman, you must. You gave your word that you would give me the list!" Sabastian said, pounding his fist on the table.

"No, Saba, I agreed to tell you where the list is because you're like a son to me. I love you, your spendthrift wife, and your overindulged children. I remember I **left** you a message on the **twenty-first** of last month. Did you get it?"

"What message? No, I didn't get a message."

"You should get a new answering machine."

"Your voice message last night said to meet you today. You promised to give me the list and the codes today. That's why I'm here. Now, please, give them to me. I have a busy schedule today."

"Yes, except I said I would tell you how to find the list and codes and, evidently more important to you, the money. Your anxiousness reminds me of a time **right** after World War II in **'46** when I got my first assignment to go to Europe. Oh, what a wonderful time that was! I **left** on **30** November and returned **right** after January, a full **sixty** days away from my students and teaching. It was worth it because that was when I began my list and the codes."

Sabastian looked around and saw Carmine bringing the plates of spaghetti with marinara sauce, a smaller plate of green beans, and a cheese grater. He placed the pasta first in front of the professor and then Sabastian. The plate of green beans went in the middle of the table.

"Parmesan, Professor?"

"Yes, please, Carmine. A double dose today."

Carmine vigorously turned the grater handle and then sprinkled the results over the professor's dish.

"Mr. Sabastian?" Carmine asked, holding the grater at the ready.

"Not much," Sabastian responded. Carmine gave the handle two slow turns and sprinkled the cheese on the plate.

"*Buon appetito*, my young friend," the professor said as he slowly wound spaghetti on his fork, using his spoon to tightly pack the pasta.

"Rodman, where can I find the list?" Sabastian asked, winding noodles on his fork with his spoon.

"Saba, are you more interested in the list and the codes or the money?"

"The list and the codes, of course," Sabastian said, looking at his plate and taking a mouthful of pasta.

"Saba, you're childlike. You can't look me in the eyes when you're lying. You tell me one minute you need the money they give you for assignments, and in the next minute, you tell me you don't care about enough money to give you freedom from them and anyone else, your own personal tenure, so to speak, compliments of our friendship, which you are here to betray."

In a tense and louder voice, Sabastian said, "If I don't leave here with the codes and list, they're going to persuade you to give them the information." Sabastian looked at Rodman as he finished these words. He was startled by how flushed the professor's neck and face were. "Professor, are you sick?" he asked.

"Saba, don't worry about me. It's just my blood pressure. This is not a pleasant experience for me. You've been the son I never had, the one I expected to train and impart with all the knowledge I've accumulated over seventy-eight years. Now you're here to tear from me the names of people who have done nothing except make their part of the world better. For what? So you and your masters can help them? I don't think so. Your new masters want to blackmail them, use them for the benefit of your masters, not their countries, or even our country. Tell me, Saba, do your masters know of the money?"

"They do."

"And how did they find out?"

"I told them," Sabastian said, looking off into the distance, "but not on purpose. They tricked me."

"I see. Is Carl still your controller?"

"Yes, why?"

"Let me guess. Carl told you they don't want the money, just the list and codes. I'll bet he said you could keep the money."

Looking amazed, Sabastian said. "Yes, he did. How did you know?"

"Saba, Saba, my stupid, naïve young friend, have you not learned anything from my tutoring all these years? Once they have the list and the codes, you're not only expendable but a detriment to them. They can't try you for embezzlement since you could tell the complete story, even about the list and codes. Dear Saba, once you've led them to the list and codes, you'll have a fatal accident or heart attack. To protect your family, you should—today—take out a large insurance policy because you're going to die soon in a way that looks like an accident or natural death."

"That's not true," Sabastian said, sitting forward with his neck outstretched, the veins protruding. He slammed his fist on the table, rattling the plates, tableware, and glasses. Patrons in the restaurant turned to look at their table. "Tell me, old man, for the love of your godchildren. Give me the list and the codes." Sabastian realized Carmine was standing to his left, slightly behind him.

"Is everything to your liking, Professor? May I be of assistance?" The calm, solid voice chilled Sabastian.

"Thank you, Carmine. Everything is fine. Saba is just excited about a new class he is teaching. Aren't you, Saba?"

"Yes. Yes, I am. I didn't mean to raise my voice. Please forgive me."

"Not a problem. Professor, I will be nearby if you need me."

"Saba, a few words of wisdom for you. First, listen more. Really listen, not just hear. Second, you must take control of your family. Be the man of the house, not someone controlled by a beautiful woman who has insatiable wants and desires for material possessions. Third, allow them to cut you off from future assignments. You're not right for the work." At that moment, Rodman's iPhone chimed. He looked down and saw the time: 1:55. "Saba, the meal is my treat. It's already on my bill. Finish your pasta. I need to go get an envelope out of the Zipcar. I'll be right back with it. It's for you." Rodman stood. His legs were wobbly. Putting both hands on the table, he steadied himself, but quickly removed them. The tingling he felt in his arms and hands was now like bee stings as his weight compressed them.

Slowly, he moved towards the front door, shuffling like an old man. He braced himself on the backs of chairs, unsure of his balance. Restaurant patrons watched with apprehension, expecting him to collapse at any moment. Some look disgusted, believing the old man had too much wine, thinking what a shame it was for someone of his age to put himself in that condition, particularly at lunch. Carmine appeared at his side and whispered, "Professor, may I be of assistance?"

"No, my dear friend, I just drank my wine too fast. I'm fine." Rodman used his remaining strength to walk the last few steps to the front door. Carmine opened the door, and Rodman walked to the small red Ford Fusion parked across the one-way street. He went to the driver's door on the street side of the car. He pretended to be feeling for his key. Looking over his right shoulder, he saw the express bus coming at the speed limit, exactly on time. He thanked God for the precision of midday buses in the city. Putting both hands on the window of the driver's door, he closed his eyes, felt the movement of air preceding the bus, and sensing the bus was at the rear of the car, pushed himself backward into the path of the bus. The impact of the bus hitting and then running over Rodman's body echoed up and down the street as well as in the restaurant, followed by the screeching of tires and wailing from bystanders.

Sabastian turned in his chair. He saw Carmine standing by the front window, leaning against the wall, his head resting on his forearm, weeping and sobbing, his chest heaving in short bursts. Patrons crowded around the front window, trying to see what happened. A woman ran through the front door screaming for someone to call 911, saying that a bus hit a man and he appeared dead. Without having to look, Sabastian knew his life had changed. He sat back in his seat, realizing he would never have the list and codes for his employers or, more importantly, the money to keep his life going. His wife would leave him. His children would suffer the humility of going to public schools. He would have to teach in some small college in the middle of nowhere for the rest of his life, all because this God-damn senile old man didn't give him the directions to the list, the codes, and the money as he'd promised. It was the first time the old man hadn't kept his promise. He hoped that mean old bastard rotted in hell.

Sabastian reached for the three books. Picking up all three, he noticed a piece of stationary sticking out of the third book. He removed the paper and unfolded it. It was a note to him from Rodman. It read:

My dear Saba,

When you read this, I will be dead—not killed by the bus because I am a coward and dislike pain. Nor do I wish to be interrogated by my former friends, who enjoy pain if it isn't their own.

The most pain I have ever felt is your betrayal. I love you like a son, but you disappoint me like an enemy. To make sure you know, I kept my word. Today at lunch, I told you where the lock box is located, the bank it is in, the box number, and the combination to the box. I told you, but you were not listening. You do not listen when you should. Now, every day of your life you will look in the mirror and know your betrayal and lack of listening caused your failure in life. Only you are responsible for that failure. I am serious about getting a large insurance policy on your life. Your new masters dislike failures.

Irving

Cinderella Dress

"HOT DAMN! WOULD Y'ALL look there!" Ryan shouted in his southern drawl. He hit the truck's steering wheel with his hand. Grinning, he looked over at Betty Sue and Jody, both craning their necks to look up through the windshield at the enormous buildings surrounding them. The three taxis in front of the Silverado, crawling to the curb under the portico of the Hilton Hotel on Sixth Avenue, stopped suddenly.

"Ryan, stop!" his fiancée Betty Sue shouted, grabbing his arm. Ryan hit the brakes, and the three of them, Ryan, Betty Sue, and Jody, his best friend for life, all lurched forward, with Betty Sue and Jody putting their hands out to brace against the dashboard. A disaster within their first few moments in New York City averted, Jody looked over at Ryan, grinning, and held out his left fist for a fist bump, careful not to brush against Betty Sue's breasts.

None of the three had ever been to New York. The three had never traveled to a city larger than Savannah, Georgia, 120 miles from their home in Lumber City, Georgia. They saw no need to go to Jacksonville, Florida, about the same distance from Lumber City as Savannah but more than twice as large and offering pro football games and concerts.

"Dude, how long did it take?" Ryan asked.

"Fourteen and a half hours. Not bad. Not bad at all, for three country bumpkins in a hot Silverado four-by-four," Jody answered. "This place is awesome."

The valet opened the truck door for Ryan. "Welcome to the Hilton. Checking in?"

"You bet."

"Great! Through the revolving doors and to the left. I'll handle your luggage for you."

"Nah, my buddy will get it." Ryan looked at Jody. "Bro, you get the bags, and I'll get the rooms. Bet, you coming with me?"

"I'm going to find the little girls' room."

"Cool. We'll meet in the lobby." Ryan took off. Jody reached into the second seat, grabbed his duffle, and put the strap across his right shoulder and under his left arm. He grabbed Ryan's bag and put it on his other shoulder. He then retrieved Betty Sue's two rollaway hard-side suitcases. Extending the handles, he placed one on each side and headed for the revolving door. He stopped. He realized he was not going through the spinning door.

The valet stepped over and held open the regular door. "This is better," he said. "Need any help with those?"

"Thanks, but no thanks. I've got them."

The valet smiled. Country-come-to-town is always the same. They hate to tip. Even when they do, it's a pittance. This crew is going on the twelfth floor, the usual place the front desk hides the hicks.

Jody entered, looked around for Ryan, and couldn't believe the lobby. It was huge, open, with a bright royal-blue circular sofa encasing a tall palm tree that reached almost to the massive crystal chandelier hanging from the high ceiling. People crowded the sofa, their luggage arrayed on the floor in front of them. Jody scanned the crowd for Ryan. He let out the whistle they used when hunting. Ryan looked around, saw him, whistled back, and started over, grinning and looking from right to left.

"Man, oh, man, isn't this something?" he drawled. "Where's Bet?"

"Don't know. I guess she's still in the bathroom."

"The elevators are this way," Ryan said, pointing to the far-right corner of the reception area. "Let's go over that way and see if the restrooms are there. Want me to carry some of that?"

"Nah, I've got it." The two of them crossed the room. Upon turning to enter the hall toward the elevators, they saw Betty Sue, just standing, apparently looking at the wall. She didn't move.

"Bet, you okay?" Ryan said.

"I'm fine," she responded, not turning to look at them. When they reached her, they saw she was looking into a room. Through the door, the only object they could see was a raised platform with a red dress on a mannequin form, the type with no head or legs. The dress had a jeweled neckline and belt and was all pleats. There were lights on all sides of the platform, shining directly on the dress from all angles. None of them had ever seen a dress like that before.

Jody walked into the room with Betty Sue quickly moving after him and Ryan reluctantly following. Once in the room, they saw a man elegantly dressed in a tailored suit, crimson tie, and white shirt, and a young woman dressed in a pale-blue blouse and navy slacks with pearls around her neck, both sitting at a table. The woman was studying a computer screen, and the man was reading a book. He put the book down, stood up, and came around to shake hands with Jody, who let loose the suitcases and duffle bags.

"Welcome, welcome! My name is Pierre Sabastian LeClec, the designer of the Cinderella Dress. Beautiful, no?" he said in accented English. "This is my assistant, Jocelyn." He turned his attention to Betty Sue. "Ah, my dear, I can see you are in love with the most beautiful dress in the world!" His eyes scanned her body from her face to her feet.

"How much is it?" Betty Sue whispered.

"Well, my dear, there is only one in this world, and there will never be another. It is priceless. And this is very important: I will only sell to the person who can wear the dress properly. If it doesn't fit, you can't buy it."

"What is the procedure for trying it on?" Jody asked as he walked around the platform, looking at the dress from all angles.

"Well, sir, there is a fee. For fifty dollars, the mademoiselle may try on the dress." As he said this, his gaze left Jody and devoured Betty Sue again.

Shyly, Betty Sue asked, "What size is it?"

"It is the perfect size," Pierre responded. "I made the dress for the most perfect female body God could create. The dress, as you can see, is all pleats. This is the challenge. Each pleat must envelop its part of the body in just the right way, expanding slightly but not too much. Many young women are beautiful in certain spots: their legs, their buttocks, their breasts, their face, one place or another. What they are not is beautiful in every place. The dress commands total beauty. That is why it is the Cinderella Dress. It will fit no one except God's perfect creation."

"Who decided what God's perfect creation is?" Jody asked, returning to stand next to Betty Sue.

"I did. It is my creation."

"Have many girls tried it on?"

"Yes. Many models, famous ones for sure, have tried on the dress, but alas, to no avail."

"How many?"

Pierre looked toward his assistant with raised eyebrows. She typed something into the computer, then looked up and said, "Fifty."

Jody did a quick calculation in his head. He turned to Betty Sue and said, "Do you want to try on the dress?"

"Yes." She turned and looked at Ryan. His eyes were studying Jocelyn like a hungry wolf studies a baby deer. "Ryan?"

"Do you have fifty dollars?" Ryan asked her.

"You know I don't have any money," she responded.

"Well, don't look at me. I don't waste money that way. Besides, what are the chances the dress will fit you? It hasn't fit those models and other women, so it's unlikely it will fit you. Come on. We need to put up our bags and get over to the arena." He picked up his bag, slung it over his shoulder, and headed for the door. At the door, he looked back at Betty Sue and Jody. "You two coming?"

Betty Sue's face burned. She looked back at the dress and turned to follow Ryan without another word. Jody slung his bag over his shoulder, extended the handles on the two suitcases and started for the door. He hesitated and turned to Pierre. "Are you here every day?"

"We will be here until five today, and here tomorrow from ten to twelve and one to five."

Jody nodded and left the room.

"Here's your key to 1207," Ryan said in front of the room. "We're right here in 1205."

"Cool. Meet downstairs in what, thirty minutes?"

"Make it forty-five. Bet may want to freshen up a bit," Ryan said, winking at Jody. Betty Sue's facial temperature rose for the second time in a few minutes.

* * *

"Mr. LeClec?" Jody asked, as he walked into room 106 off the lobby. Jocelyn smiled as she looked up, sitting taller in her chair and closing her laptop. She unbuttoned the top button on her blouse.

"Ah, yes, sir. Welcome back. I deeply apologize, sir. I didn't get your name earlier," LeClec responded.

"Jody. Jody's fine. I'd like to cut a deal with you." LeClec was standing behind the table and came around to stand in front of Jody. Jocelyn sat back and crossed her arms just below her breasts, smiling.

"How may I assist you?"

Jody reached into his front jeans pocket and pulled out two twenties and a ten. "I'd like to pay for my friend to try on the dress, on one condition."

"What condition might that be?"

"You tell my friend she can try on the dress for free. You don't tell her or anyone else I paid the money."

"Why?"

"Because. Just because. Do we have a deal or not?"

LeClec looked at Jocelyn, looked back at Jody, then said, "Deal." He held out his hand for the money.

"They're staying in room 1205. We're here today and tomorrow, leaving early the next day. I thought you could have the hotel tell them this evening and she could try it on tomorrow."

"Perfect. I'll arrange a special invitation."

* * *

"Look at this place! There are fifty lanes set up! Holy shit, this is awesome!" Ryan turned in circles just inside the Javits

Center. The staff had set it up for the international tournament of NATF, the National Axe Throwing Federation. Ryan and Jody were the regional champions from the Southeast US. Jody was the individual champion, with Ryan as runner-up, and they were the team champions as well. Ryan and Jody fist bumped. Betty Sue gazed at the enormous open arena with her fingers in her ears.

"Where's the custom axe maker?" Jody asked.

Ryan surveyed the arena and saw a large sign down the aisle leading to the back of the room. "Back there. Let's go." He grabbed Betty Sue's hand.

Jody followed, looking from side to side at the lanes. Some contestants were already practicing for the big day tomorrow. The throwers he saw impressed him. Tough competition, he thought, except throwing today ain't like throwing tomorrow, when all the dough is on the line. That's when the men cut out the boys. Jody smiled.

The guy behind the table was sharpening an axe when they walked up. He continued to lightly touch the blade against the stone on a foot-pedal-controlled spinning wheel. "What can I do for you?" the man asked without looking up.

"We're looking for Red Lanier," Ryan said. The man stopped spinning the wheel, blew on the axe head, and wiped it with a cloth. He looked up, first taking in Betty Sue and then Ryan.

"That's me, dude. And you are?"

"Ryan Hotchkiss. This here is my friend, Jody Hotchkiss. I'm the one who made an appointment with you to get a new set of custom axes before the tournament."

"Oh, yeah, from Georgia. You're in the right place. Brothers throwing together. Don't see that often."

"Well, we're not actually brothers. They say we're brothers from different mothers and fathers. Our fathers are brothers, and our mothers are friends. We grew up as close families, so maybe some people would call us brothers," Jody explained. "This is Betty Sue Sovey, our partner in crime."

"That's almost too much info. You have the money?" Red said, looking at Ryan.

"Got it right here," he said, patting his pocket.

"Let's get started. It'll take two hours each to do it right."

"I'm going to pass," Jody said.

"I'd like to go back to the hotel and rest," Betty Sue said to Ryan.

"Bet, I don't have time to take you back. Can't you just hang here?"

"Give me the keys and I'll take her back while you get outfitted. I'll be back, and we can scope out the place and competition," Jody said, holding out his hand.

"That's cool," Ryan said. "Don't get into any trouble, Bet. We'll be back by five. Big night in the big city tonight." He turned back to Lanier. "Let's get started, man."

Neither spoke on the way back to the hotel. The pressure to speak, however, built steadily. Jody wanted to suggest she go back to room 106 but knew she was too bright to buy the ruse if he did. There were so many things to say, but the fear of one or the other telling Ryan, even by accident, stopped them. The silence burst when Jody stopped the truck at the curb on Sixth Avenue.

"There's a museum right down the street that way," Jody said, pointing to his right, across her body. "It's got some weird stuff but also some pretty awesome stuff, too. You ought to check it out. We'll be back by five."

Betty Sue, with her hand on the truck door handle, looked at Jody. "How do you know that? You've never been here before."

Jody blushed. "I read up about what was around the hotel before we came."

"Why?" Betty Sue took her hand off the handle and turned to face Jody. "Pull over there for a minute," she said, pointing to the curb under the hotel portico.

He eased into the driveway. Looking at her, he felt his heart skip a beat and looked back through the windshield. He took a deep breath. "One day—I don't know when—I'm moving up here. This city is alive. It pulsates with opportunities and ideas. I want to be part of it. I know I can make something of myself up here. Do you understand?" He looked back at her.

"Yeah, somewhat. I read every fashion magazine I can. This is a glamorous life, for sure. But what's wrong with home? You're doing pretty good at the mill. You're in accounting, not on a machine doing shift work."

"I'll still be working at the mill when I retire if I stay at home. I want to do something besides wait for a paycheck each week, with everyone from the government on down taking a piece of me and my time before I get my cut. There's more to life than that. Don't you ever dream of leaving and going somewhere bigger, brighter, and more interesting than Jeff Davis County?"

"I know Ryan will never leave Lumber City."

"That doesn't mean you can't. You didn't answer my question. Do you ever dream of leaving, getting a modeling job, making it in a place like this?"

"Sometimes I do. I like home. It's a safe place, a part of me. But yeah, I do dream." She looked away from Jody and at the stream of people entering and leaving the lobby. "I've got to go." She opened the truck door, slammed it, and walked into the hotel.

Betty Sue looked around the lobby. The circular sofa had no unoccupied space. Children ran in and around the suitcases that sat helter-skelter in front of the tourists as they milled around. Tourist lines reached almost to the center of the room, waiting to check in with one of the five receptionists. Betty Sue headed to the elevators. In the hall, she looked to her left and saw the dress still on the pedestal, engulfed in the bright lights.

Over her shoulder, she heard someone say, "Hi." She looked, and it was Jocelyn.

"You're Betty Sue from Georgia, right?"

"Yeah."

"I'm glad I ran into you. Pierre, Mr. LeClec, wanted to speak with you. He's on the phone but will be free in a couple of minutes. Do you have a minute? He really wants to see you."

As the two women entered the room, LeClec looked up and quickly finished his call. "Welcome, my young friend. Come in, come in. I decided after you left earlier—yes, I have—I want you to try on the Cinderella Dress. There will be no charge. It is my gift to your beauty. You agree, yes? Of course, you do. Come, Jocelyn will assist you. Yes, she will." He motioned for Betty Sue and Jocelyn to go to the dressing enclosure. "I'll get the cameras ready."

"You'll have to remove all of your clothes. Would you like me to assist you or turn my back, so you'll have privacy?"

"Everything, really? Even my bra and panties?"

"I'm afraid so. The dress drapes over the body. That's why it doesn't fit most people. "Their bodies look wonderful with help from their garments but not from nature. Mr. LeClec created the dress to fit the mythical body of Venus or at least what he considers the perfect proportions of a woman."

"Whatever." Betty Sue reached under her plaid shirt and unfastened her bra, pulled it away from one arm and then the other, and handed it to Jocelyn, who folded it carefully and placed it on the table. Still wearing her shirt, Betty Sue unzipped her jeans. After kicking off her boots, she bent at the waist, hooked her thumbs on either side of the jeans and her panties, pulled them down, and stepped out of them. Jocelyn was holding the dress up so that Betty Sue was not visible to her and the dress would slip over Betty Sue's head. Betty Sue dropped the shirt and stepped into the dress, feeling its silky, cool fabric conform to her body. Jocelyn stepped around Betty Sue and zipped the dress. She then handed Betty Sue the belt.

"This belt looks almost real."

"That's because these are not rhinestones. They are tiny, individually set diamonds. So is the collar." Jocelyn stepped back and surveyed Betty Sue. She adjusted the dress at the shoulders. "There. Let's go to the platform."

"Belle. Absolument magnifique," LeClec muttered under his breath. "Please step up and stand on the tape marks." He held out his hand for her. "Absolument magnifique," he whispered again. "Jocelyn, the cameras are ready." He backed away to the table. Jocelyn clicked the computer keys.

LeClec walked back over to Betty Sue. "My dear, please place your right foot here, leaving the left where it is," he pointed to a spot just to the front of her left foot. "That's it. Now, allow your arms to relax by your sides as you move your shoulders down and back. Parfaite! You will be a successful model, for sure. Now, Jocelyn, we are ready."

Jocelyn clicked the laptop keyboard. All at once, the lights surrounding Betty Sue exploded in brightness, and then it was over. Betty Sue didn't move. "The photos are complete, my dear. You may relax and step down. Here, let me help you." Again, LeClec held out his hand. When she was down, he didn't let go. Instead, he rubbed her hand slowly and seductively. "Have you modeled before in your hometown? Anywhere?"

Betty Sue blushed. "No, never. Nowhere."

"You are a natural. I would like to discuss a modeling contract with you."

"I don't know," she stammered. "I really don't have time."

"But you must make time. You will be a sensation. It will take a few months to train you, but you will be on the cover of every fashion magazine within a year. I've never in my life seen such raw talent and beauty."

She pulled her hand from his. "Really, I've got to go. I'll be late. Thanks for the opportunity to try on the dress."

"Betty Sue, give me your cell number," Jocelyn directed.

"What do you need it for?" Betty Sue looked, wide-eyed, at Jocelyn.

"So I can send you these pictures. You need to see and keep them."

"I don't want them."

"Yes, you do." Jocelyn looked directly at Betty Sue. Betty Sue saw the friendliness in her eyes. She wanted the photos. She knew she looked good in them, but Ryan would go berserk if he saw she tried on the dress. They had to be sent elsewhere rather than her phone. Ryan often randomly took it out of her pocket or bag and flipped through it, looking at who she'd called or texted. It infuriated her, but Ryan was Ryan.

"Okay." She rattled off Jody's cell number. She would have to alert Jody that the photos were coming. He'd understand not to tell Ryan, she hoped.

Jocelyn unzipped the dress. With no regard for modesty, Betty Sue allowed Jocelyn to pull it over her head. Betty Sue reached for her bra and panties on the table. "Are both guys your boyfriends or just the bad boy?"

"No. What do you mean 'the bad boy'?"

"One of them treats you like dirt or an object he possesses. The other is in love with you in such a way he idolizes you."

"No, you're wrong. Ryan is my boyfriend. We've been together since the seventh grade. He loves me. The other guy, in the red T-shirt, is his best friend and my friend as well. The three of us hang out together. At home they call us the Three Musketeers. Me and Jody are friends, that's all."

"Really? I've got news for you. You can't let LeClec know I told you or I may get fired. The one you call just a friend—I think you said his name is Joseph, no?"

"Jody."

"Yes, Jody. He paid for you to try on the dress. He didn't want you or your boyfriend to know. You can say what you want, but he's in love with you, of that I'm certain. While I'm speaking so bluntly, I've got two pieces of advice for you. First, beware of Pierre. You are a piece of meat to him. The first thing he wants to do is get you in his bed. While that is fun, to him it is just domination, sort of like your bad boy. Pierre is serious about you having the talent to go far in the modeling world, and he can make you a star model, but the price he extracts will be high in the long run. Be careful and hear what I'm saying if you take him up on his offer."

Betty Sue half listened as she continued dressing.

"Second, your bad boy. I don't know why—yes, I do. Young girls all go for the bad boys. It's in the DNA, I guess. I was just like you when I was your age. I had me a bad boy, twice, in fact. The first time, I didn't know better. The second time, I was stupid. Both treated me the same as your bad boy, and it got worse as time went on. In both cases, I became pregnant. In both cases, they went looking for someone new without the baggage of children. I love my children and thank God for them every day, but it's no fun being a single mom. Bad boys want the fun and not the responsibility. I've given you friendly advice. I doubt you've heard it, but at least you now know. Now, if you have no interest in him, please let—what's his name—Jody, that's it, know I'd really like to get to know him better. A lot better." Jocelyn smiled at Betty Sue.

In the hallway, Betty Sue hesitated. She looked to her left at the elevators. Turning right, she left the hotel. When the light turned green, she walked to the east, her thoughts jumbled and coming like a summer afternoon storm in South Georgia. Jody had said there was a museum down this street. She saw MOMA and started in. She realized she had no money, so she decided walking and thinking were the answers. Could LeClec do what he said he could: get her into real modeling? He said she would be on the covers of Elle, Vogue, Vanity Fair, Cosmo, and W. Fame could be hers. But he'd want her to have sex with him, and God knows who else she'd have to sleep with. Betty Sue shuddered. She had never had sex with anyone but Ryan because she loved him.

She kept walking, watching the working people as they sat on the sidewalk, eating their food cart lunches and watching her and the other people walking by. The cars and trucks were creeping down the street when possible. The noise of the city—voices, clanging, and honking—all signified that the city was alive. When she reached Fifth Avenue, she stopped, looking at a larger crowd of people that moved like a snake, going both ways. She turned to the right, planning to go up to Fifty-Third Street and then back to the hotel. The shop windows caught her eyes. The first store's diamonds, rubies, emeralds, and sapphires encased in yellow and white gold bracelets, earrings, necklaces, and rings brought her mind back to the Cinderella Dress and LeClec. She envisioned wearing real jewelry. Yeah, if she became a model, she could.

Betty Sue pictured herself as a successful model. She held that thought as she walked. Looking at the clothes, she pictured herself modeling them. Her stride changed to a runway walk she'd learned from a video on YouTube she had watched every night for over a year. She could be a model, she told herself. Her mind thought about the luxuries she could have, the places she could go, the people she could meet, the life she could lead. Instead of turning at Fifty-Third Street, she continued down Fifth Avenue, looking in each store window, picturing herself modeling the clothes. She turned at Fifty-Second Street, heading back to the hotel and perhaps a different life.

* * *

"Dude, you ready?" Ryan asked, standing in front of 1207.

"I'll meet y'all downstairs in ten! Running late!" Jody hollered through the door. He was sitting in his boxers on the bed, looking at his phone. He had seen nothing as arousing as the photos of Betty Sue in the red dress. Why did she send the photos to him? Did LeClec tell her he had paid for the try-on? Did Betty Sue have a copy? Had Ryan seen them? Jesus, she was beautiful. How could she put on a dress and turn into the most beautiful woman he'd ever seen? Jody sent the photos to his computer. Ryan had a habit of borrowing his phone, so they couldn't stay on it. He deleted the photos from the phone and got dressed. He hung the Do Not Disturb sign on the door and headed to the elevators.

"You guys ready to party?"

"Waiting on you, bro," Ryan responded. "I'll get them to bring around the truck."

"No way. We're going to do some serious eating and drinking. None of us want to end up in jail. We're going to take what they affectionately call a 'yellow chariot.' We Georgia rednecks call them taxis."

Ryan got in first, Betty Sue second, and Jody last. The valet held the door open, waiting for a tip. Jody just smiled at him and pulled the door shut.

"Where to, guys?"

"Gansevoort and Tenth Avenue, please."

The driver turned the meter on, then looked in the rearview mirror and said in a Middle Eastern accent, "Where's that?"

Jody leaned forward, placing his hand on Betty Sue's knee for balance. "Take a left onto Sixth Avenue and another left at Fifty-Fifth. Go down to Ninth Avenue, take another left, and when you get to Gansevoort, take a right and go one block."

"Yes, sir," the driver said, disappointment in his voice. Jody sat back, a smile on his face. He avoided looking at Betty Sue and took his hand off her knee. The three of them were one, with their thighs touching.

"That was awesome, dude. How d'you know that?" Ryan said in a low voice and held out his right fist for a fist bump.

"Up here, you'd better know how to get where you want to go, or else you'll end up touring the city for a lot of money. I just Googled the area where we can find some action. We're going to where the action is." He bumped Ryan's fist and sat back, looking out the window, trying not to think of the pictures he'd seen.

Betty Sue closed her eyes. She could feel the electricity coursing through her body from the two guys. She realized she had never felt the connection with Jody before. In the cab, his presence and energy were greater than Ryan's. Was Jocelyn right? It couldn't be, but she felt his touch for the first time. Had he looked at the pictures? What did he think about them? She had to explain to him. A shiver involuntarily rolled through her body.

"You cold, Bet?" Ryan asked.

"No, I'm good."

"I know that," he responded, squeezing her leg. She moved his hand.

* * *

"It'll be forty minutes' wait time; you can sit at the bar and I'll call you," the perky hostess said, having scanned the three of them and let her gaze rest on Ryan.

"Cool," Ryan responded, giving the hostess his best South Georgia smile and drawl. The three of them snagged a high topper at the edge of the packed bar. The din of voices, mixed with the thumping beat from the music somehow contained primarily to the bar area, made it difficult to carry on a conversation. After ordering a round of Coors Light, Ryan leaned in and said, "I'm going to go find the bathroom." With that, he got up, grabbing a beer from the approaching server, and inched his way sideways through the crowd. Jody, sliding his stool closer to Betty Sue, leaned over toward her.

"Why'd you—" Betty Sue and Jody said in unison. They both laughed.

"You go first," Jody said.

"No, you first," Betty Sue responded.

"Ladies first, in all things," Jody said, holding out his hand to her.

"Why'd you pay for me to try on the dress?"

"That asshole promised not to tell," Jody snapped, shaking his head from side to side, reaching for the beer just delivered.

"Pierre didn't tell me; Jocelyn did. And that's not all she said."

"What else was there to be said? Anyway, why did you send the photos to me?"

"You got the photos because you paid for the shit. That's a lie." Betty Sue took a long swig of her beer, put it down, and looked off to the right. She turned back to look directly at Jody, locking eye contact. "I sent them to you because I couldn't send them to my phone. You know why."

"I figured as much. No sweat. I sent them to my computer and deleted them from my phone. Sometimes he does the same thing to me. Have you seen them?"

"No. But the dress fit. LeClec was beside himself."

"I bet. He probably had a boner from the second you put it on, if he's not too old."

"He's not too old. He offered me a modeling job with his design house, said I could be the modeling sensation of the fashion world within a couple of years. Jocelyn said he could make me a real deal. She also said I'd have to be his mistress if I took the offer."

"Betty Sue, forget the mistress part for a second. This is your chance at a glamorous life, doing what you've dreamed about. I've always known you could be more than a Lumber City girl. Are you going to talk seriously with him?"

"Jesus, I don't know. It's happening too fast. I've got to have time to think about it. Right now, I'm about to throw up just thinking of telling Ryan about leaving and moving to New York. Besides, I don't know anybody here, and it's humongous and scary. I walked around the block, up to Fifth Avenue, down to Fifty-Second, and back to Sixth, and I saw more people than there are in Lumber City. I can't get my head around the idea."

"You know someone living up here."

"Who?"

"Me. I've decided that if we win tomorrow, I'm taking my half, putting it with my savings, and using my 401(k) as a backup so I can move up here." Jody looked at Betty Sue for a reaction. She lowered her eyes, clutching her beer bottle with both hands.

"What's the matter? Do you think it's a completely crazy idea?"

"No, that's not it." Taking a deep breath, smiling, and looking up and around to make sure Ryan wasn't approaching, she said, "It's the other thing Jocelyn said. She said you're in love with me. She could see it in your eyes the first time we were in the room and the second time when you came to make the deal with Pierre. Is there any truth to that?"

Jody couldn't look at Betty Sue. He didn't know how to handle the fact that his feelings were so obvious. So much for becoming a professional poker player. He looked down at his beer. "You belong to Ryan. Ryan is my brother by another mother. It doesn't matter what I am or am not."

"I'm not owned by anyone!" Betty Sue snapped.

"You know what I mean. You and Ryan have been together since the seventh grade. It doesn't matter what my feelings for you are. If we're in Lumber City, you're Ryan's girl. I'll be living in New York in about six weeks if we win. If you want to move to New York, I'll be here. You won't be alone. You won't have to fuck LeClec, either. He lost his edge over you by telling the truth. You are beautiful. If he can see it instantly, so can others. You can get a job with a first-class modeling agency. Hell, I got a boner just looking at the photos. Those photos can be your ticket and I can help. Yeah, I love you. I'm not ashamed of it, but in Lumber City, there isn't a goddamn thing I can do about it."

"I didn't know."

"Now you do. Now you have choices in your life. That may be scary to you, but it is a choice."

Betty Sue looked around. "Where is he, anyway? It doesn't take that long to pee."

"He's over by the bar, talking to some people." Jody cocked his head toward the bar.

"I need another beer. See if you can get the server's attention," Betty Sue said before draining her Coors. "That's one thing about Ryan," she added, "he never meets a stranger, particularly if they wear a skirt."

"Well, before he comes back, remember you now have choices in your life," Jody said, signaling for the server.

* * *

Ryan, Betty Sue, and Jody walked into the Javits Center at 1:00 p.m. the next day. All three wore their standard uniforms:

roper boots, blue jeans, and a T-shirt. Betty Sue's jeans were tight and so was her T-shirt. Jody carried his set of axes in a canvas bag, the strap thrown over his shoulder. Ryan scanned the cavernous hall for Red Lanier's sign. Betty Sue held her fingers to her ears. Seeing Lanier's sign high on the back wall, Ryan headed that way, with Jody and Betty Sue following.

"They ready?" Ryan asked as he shook hands with Red.

"Yep." Red reached under the table and pulled out a canvas bag with his name in big red letters on both sides. He extracted three hatchets from the bag and laid them out on the brown felt table covering. The heads gleamed in the bright lights. The handles were a dark-colored hardwood, different from the standard hatchets available everywhere else, and one had a red-painted grip. "This one is your practice axe. The head weighs a half-pound more than the others, both of which are only one ounce above the minimum acceptable weight of one and a quarter pounds. The practice axe is a half-ounce less than the maximum weight of one and three-quarter pounds, so you can still use it in competition in case one of the other two breaks."

"Awesome," Ryan whispered as he picked up a hatchet, turning it over and over in his hands. Jody picked up the practice hatchet, surveying the sharpness by gliding it over his arm. Hair accumulated on the blade, leaving his arm smooth. He wiped the blade on his pants leg.

Betty Sue watched the two of them, her eyes darting back and forth, spending more time on Jody than Ryan.

The National Axe Throwing Federation, known as the NATF, not to be confused with the United States ATF authorities, started in Toronto, Canada, and spread rapidly across Canada, the United States, Poland, and Southeast Asia, including Australia, Singapore, Thailand, and South Korea. Maybe it was the social or political times, but it appealed to a certain element in society. Axe throwing is not for the faint of heart, nor for heavy drinkers, nor for the metrosexual male. While some people enjoy rolling a twelve-pound ball down a lane to strike pins and others enjoy throwing miniature pointed missiles at a cork circle, the bar attendee who has a self-image of a rough-and-tumble guy or gal finds some deep satisfaction in trying to stick a hatchet in two-by-ten wooden boards with circles drawn on them. The rules of the sport are quite rigorous: any thrower must agree to a one-drink-per-hour limit, no hard liquor, throwing lanes that protect the participants and spectators, and specific rules covering all aspects of competition.

The Javits Center main hall was set up in twenty arenas, four lanes of targets considered appropriate for teams of two contenders each. It looked the same as in most competitions, heavy-gauge chain-link fencing reached fifteen feet high on the outsides of each set of two lanes, with six-foot, same-thickness chain-link fence between the two throwing lanes of contestants. There were four lines drawn across each lane: a solid red line denoting the farthest any person can go while a contestant is preparing to throw, a solid black line from which a throw happens, a dotted blue line used only for a tied match when the big axe throw-off is necessary to break the tie, and a yellow line to keep spectators from getting too close to the action.

Each match was comprised of three rounds, in which the contestants threw five times at the target. A bull's-eye counted for five points, so the maximum score per round was twenty-five, with one exception: on each target was a 2.625-inch green circle in the upper right and left corners of the target. A player could call, "Clutch!" prior to a throw, and if the axe hit and stuck in one of the green circles, it counted for seven points. The bull's-eye on the standard target was seven inches in diameter. "Clutch!" is usually a choice of last resort.

Anytime one team could not win mathematically, the match was over. With fifteen throws in a match, a long competition separated the champion players from the field. As in most, if not all, competitive fields, mental conditioning was more important than physical fitness. There exists no past or future for a competing champion, only the precise seconds they are performing. Champions don't allow thoughts about anyone else to clutter their minds during competition. There are no random recollections of a past poor throw or yearning for the prize money or standing in the winner's circle, just the precise physical movement necessary to accomplish the task. Ryan and Jody had honed this mental skill all their lives hunting in the woods and swamps at home.

"The teams to beat," Ryan said while setting up in their assigned arena, "are the fellas from Mississippi and Toronto."

"Bullshit," Jody retorted. "The team to beat is from Lumber City, Georgia." He held out his fist for a bump.

"Bet, here's twenty dollars. How about seeing if you can find us a sports drink and some snacks?" Ryan directed.

"Sure."

Competition started at 2:00 p.m. Ryan and Jody didn't complete a full match all afternoon, throwing perfect scores in each round, while their competition became more erratic as the time wore on. Word of the guys from Georgia spread, and the crowd watching Ryan and Jody began building with each successful match. Finally, the officials called a thirty-minute break while they cleared the hall of arenas other than the one to be used by the two remaining teams: Toronto and Lumber City.

"Hey, dude, what are you going to do with your half of the fifteen-thousand dollars of first-prize money?" Ryan asked Jody. Betty Sue watched Jody to see if he would tell Ryan about his plans to move to New York City.

Jody caught Betty Sue's eye and smiled. "Man, I'm not even thinking about that. What did our daddies tell us, 'Don't spend any money you don't have in your hand'?" Jody looked away and changed the subject. "It sure looks like it's going to be a party. Man, I've never seen so many good-looking girls in one place in my life. Not as pretty as you, Betty Sue, but still awesome."

"You fellas ready?" The official came over to Ryan and Jody, followed by two bearded twenty-something guys from Toronto. Both had on boots, jeans, and T-shirts with a Canadian flag and the word Toronto emblazoned across the front and back.

"Yes, sir."

"Introduce yourselves while I finish the paperwork. One contestant from each team does Rock Paper Scissors to see who selects a lane first. Both team members of the winner get to select the starting lanes. After each round, you'll rotate the lanes. In the event of a tied round, we will accept the tie until the last round. Only in the last round will there be a big axe throw-off. Everybody understand the rules?"

"Yes, sir," the four contestants said in unison.

"Let's get started."

The Toronto team of Brian and Tony won the right to select the lanes for the first round. The spectator crowd swelled to six deep on the sides, and the bleachers behind the contestants were full. Heckling began immediately, mostly directed toward the Lumber City throwers. Round one ended with a perfect round for both teams, accumulating twenty-five points each. The second round repeated the first round, with each thrower on the mark. In the third round, the first three throws by each participant were perfect.

On the fourth throw, the Toronto team was perfect. Ryan's throw was dead center. Jody stepped to the black line, staring at the target. In a split second, and only for less than a second, he thought about Betty Sue in the Cinderella Dress. He let the axe fly, and it was high, cutting into the bull's-eye and the red ring. The crowd let out a groan and then started singing the Canadian national anthem.

Ryan looked at the official and hollered, "Device!" The lane official turned to the match official and repeated the call for the device. The device was a set of calipers used to measure the amount of the axe that is contained in each part of the target, measuring from the outside of the painted portion of the target representing the highest score. Jody and Ryan stood at the red line, facing the crowd with their backs to the target to prevent anyone from going near the target. The officials arrived with the device, and the two contestants stepped aside. Three officials looked, measured, looked again, measured again, conferred among themselves, and shook their heads. The lead official stepped forward and hollered, "Bull's-eye!" A loud groan went up from the partisan crowd.

The last throw. Brian of the Toronto team went first and threw a bull's-eye. Jody was next and threw a bull's-eye. Tony from Toronto went third and threw a bull's-eye. The spectators broke out in cheers and stomped their feet. Ryan walked up to the black line. He looked at his new hatchet lying on the table and reached for it. Stopping, his hand just inches away from the axe, he turned. The spectators went silent as Ryan walked over to where Betty Sue was standing. He grabbed her and gave her a passionate kiss. The crowd roared. She kissed him back, raising her right leg and cocking it behind his legs. Another roar went up from the crowd.

Ryan turned and hollered, "Clutch!" The lane official echoed his call. The crowd went silent. Ryan walked to the black line, and, like a river flowing, never hesitated, picking up his instrument and throwing it at the upper right 2.625-inch green dot on the target. The hatchet hit solidly and sliced the circle in half. There was a moment of stunned silence and then a rising crescendo of *The Star-Spangled Banner*.

* * *

Jody watched from the corner of the area cleared for dancing as the mass of writhing bodies pulsated to the beat of the music. He touched his jeans pocket again, just to make sure the check was still there. He watched Ryan and Betty Sue dancing. Back home, their friends called it safe sex. He made his way over to the lane where he had left his bag, retrieved it, slung it over his shoulder, and made his way out of the Javits Center. It seemed like an enjoyable night for a walk to the hotel, he mused, as he stepped off the curb, headed to Sixth Avenue.

Lucky

O H, GOD, I'M NOT dressed properly, Adrienne thought as she maneuvered her thirty-five-year-old VW Beetle onto the parking deck, looking through the windshield at the people in white shorts, multicolored shirts, and Lilly Pulitzer sundresses. She turned off the engine, got out, and tugged down her gray T-shirt with the slogan "Give Me Head or Nothing at All" on the front, trying to cover the space between her jeans and the ragged end of the shirt, which she had deliberately ripped years ago so the piercing in her belly button would show. Walking toward the gleaming white-stucco and red-tile-roofed beach club, she muttered to herself, "It's not my fault. It's not my fault." On either side of the massive double-door entrance were shiny brass plaques. The one on the left read "The Beach Club"; the one on the right, "Private Members and Guests Only."

Walking through the doors, she saw the attendant at the welcome desk. "May I help you?" the attendant said, looking Adrienne up and down with a frown on her face.

"I'm Adrienne Wilson, here to see Mr. Allister Crumby."

"Is Mr. Crumby expecting you?"

"Of course. Is he here?" Adrienne said, disdain in her voice.

Pointing over Adrienne's left shoulder, the attendant responded, "Take the double doors and walk to the front of the veranda. You'll find him there at the outside, southernmost table." The attendant looked down at her computer, dismissing Adrienne.

The elderly man stood when he saw Adrienne approaching. He wore white pants, a blue striped shirt, a red tie, a navy-blue double-breasted sport coat, and black loafers without socks. Leaning against the table was a black cane with a sterling silver handle. A straw planter's hat was hanging on the back post of his chair. Holding out his hand, he said, "Ms. Wilson, welcome to the Beach Club. Please have a seat." He held out the chair for her. He took his seat, looked over to the server, and nodded. The server approached the table and filled Adrienne's water glass.

"Coffee?" the uniformed young lady asked.

"No. Tea and an English muffin," Adrienne said, looking out at the ocean, past the mandevilla vines, hibiscus flowers, and palm trees. She knew this way of life was what she wanted.

The server looked at the elderly gentleman. "Mr. Crumby, will you have the usual?"

Looking at the server, he said, "Yes, Vivian, two scrambled egg whites, real crisp bacon, grits, and an English muffin, please. Thank you."

"Yes, sir," Vivian said, smiling.

Turning to Adrienne, Crumby smiled and said, "Now, Ms. Wilson, may I call you Adrienne?"

"Yes. It's not my fault," Adrienne blurted out, looking down at her teacup and then off to her right at the ocean. The ocean looked just as she felt, in turmoil. The stiff breeze blowing from the ENE and the tide going out were two forces of nature competing, creating whitecaps and waves. She wondered why she was sitting there, talking with this ancient man who has more wrinkles than a dried prune? She turned back toward the man and smiled.

"How is your grandfather?" he asked. "I haven't seen him in a couple of weeks."

"He's good. He said to say hello and thanks you for seeing me."

"My dear, why don't you start at the beginning so I can understand and perhaps help?" Crumby said softly with a smile. "Are you sure you don't want a proper breakfast, along with the tea and English muffin?"

"No, thank you. The beginning? You mean that evening when I got the phone call in the newsroom?"

"No, Adrienne, the beginning. I want to know step-by-step how you realized you wanted to be a journalist," Crumby said as he poured honey in his teapot. "I've got all day, so take your time. Give me all the details. If you need my help, I've got to understand everything."

Damn, I don't have all day, she thought. Granddaddy said he could help me, not be my confessor. "You mean in college?"

"No, I mean from the very first. Did you want to be a journalist in the first grade? Fifth grade? When?" Crumby was smiling and his voice was soft, but Adrienne heard the hint of exasperation in his voice. He sat back with an irritating air of success and confidence she had seen people in their 70s and 80s bring to serious conversations with young people. What made it more irritating was that the young adults were just finding out life isn't fair, full of luck, forgiving, nor character- ized by any of the other positive emotions and perspectives their parents and teachers told them were their birthright.

"I don't want to waste your time," she said, hoping he would relent.

"My dear, your grandfather is a good friend of mine. He asked me to help you. I must understand how I can help because I don't have a magic wand. I have all day. At my age, that's common. If you are in a rush to get on with your life, do so. It has been a pleasure meeting you. I wish you well." He picked up his teacup, all the time keeping his eyes focused on hers. He could see the glint of moisture as she blinked rapidly.

"Yes, sir—eh, I mean, no, sir. I'm not in a hurry. I just didn't want to impose on you."

"You're not imposing. This is a lovely spot to pass the time away. If we get stiff sitting, we can go for a walk along the Spit, see the erosion they say is not happening, and then come back. Now, please, from the beginning."

"I was a sophomore in high school. I was a cheerleader in a group of popular girls, all cheerleaders who were interested in fashion and boys—not necessarily in that order," Adrienne said, smiling at Crumby. "My English teacher, Mr. Saben, wanted to have a program during the New Year's School Assembly in January. This assembly is when all the students rededicate themselves to finishing the school year with their best efforts. Everyone in Mr. Saben's class came up with a project to present at the assembly, and he picked mine for presentation. My proposal was about the political gridlock in Washington and its effects on our school and community. I was enthralled with the project." Adrienne became animated as she talked about her high school life after the project. "I dropped out of cheerleading and started working on the school newspaper. Mr. Saben was the advisor for both the newspaper and yearbook. I loved it. I became the gossip columnist, covered the dances, and even took up photography my junior year.

"By my senior year, I knew I wanted to go to journalism school in college. Mr. Saben helped me select four colleges, and I applied to three and was wait-listed at all three. Mr. Saben had a friend at the Crumby School of Journalism at the state university. He called his friend and found out the standard requirements for journalism schools were a 3.75 GPA and a two-thousand-word essay about why the student wanted to be a journalist. My grade point average was 3.5, so I was lucky in that Mr. Saben gave me some makeup assignments and credit for working on the newspaper, then went back and changed my

English grades for the last three years to bring my overall GPA up to 3.75. He also helped me draft an essay that would hit all the important points his friend said were necessary. Pretty lucky, eh? If he hadn't called, I would have failed to get into that school as well," Adrienne said, looking at Crumby and winking. Her eyes widened. "Oh, my God, I just realized the connection. The Crumby School, and your name is Crumby. Was it named after your grandfather, father, or uncle?"

"Not exactly, my dear. They named it after me. I was lucky enough to have the resources to give them a gift to construct the building and endow three distinguished professor chairs."

"Awesome," Adrienne said as she took a bite of her muffin and a sip of tea. *Maybe he can help me.*

"So, you magically had a 3.75 GPA and wrote a—what do young people say—an awesome essay with the help of your English teacher? Go on, this is interesting."

"Well, I got an early acceptance at Crumby School. I was both excited and apprehensive…"

Crumby interrupted, "Excuse me. What do you mean, apprehensive? Please explain."

"What I mean is because it wasn't exactly my essay, and I didn't exactly get a 3.75 GPA, I was, you know, apprehensive, worried about making it, concerned. Mr. Saben said that didn't matter really. He said what mattered was getting in and graduating with the diploma. He said it didn't matter if I was at the top of the class or the bottom of the class. Only the Crumby diploma on the resumé mattered. I wasn't comfortable, but he said I would make a talented journalist," Adrienne said, twisting her hands around her napkin and looking off toward the ocean.

"So, you got lucky, thanks to Mr. Saben, and went to Crumby School. Go on. This is interesting, how people manipulate the system. What journalistic focus did you choose?" He shifted slightly in his chair, crossing his right leg over his left.

"Politics. The work I had done for the school assembly made me realize there was an exciting career opportunity in the political field, not just working for a media outlet but also for writing books. I had—have—no interest in sports, business, crime, or lifestyle reporting. To me, all these other areas are like planets orbiting around the sun of politics. The political class has become the aristocracy of the United States since the turn of the twentieth century."

"That's an interesting observation. Most young people don't see that obvious truth." Crumby pushed back from the table, turning his chair slightly so he was facing to Adrienne's right, toward the ocean. He turned his head to his right to look at her and crossed his legs. With a nod, he signaled for Vivian to come over to their table. "You may clear these dishes," he said, pointing to his breakfast plates. "May I have some hot water for my teapot, please?" he asked. Looking at Adrienne, he asked, "Would you like another muffin or more tea, my dear?"

"No, thank you, but if you'll excuse me, I'll go to the restroom," she said, standing. Crumby started to rise and Adrienne said, "Please don't get up."

"It's no bother being a gentleman, Adrienne," Crumby said, standing, pointing out the direction to the restrooms, then taking his seat as she walked away. The server brought a pot of hot water with fresh tea bags. Crumby added honey to his teacup and poured the hot tea into the cup. He knew how this story ended. She was smart but not brilliant. She didn't have much street sense. That's the problem with young people: their families sheltered them from life and didn't allow them to get their noses bloody growing up. How sad. He took a sip of tea while looking off at the ocean, enjoying the stiff breeze and rough waves. Adrienne returned to the table. Crumby stood while she took her seat.

"Tell me," Crumby asked, "who was your advisor at journalism school?"

"I was lucky. My freshman year, Mr. Rahani, who was from India, was my advisor. He was finishing his PhD and working on his thesis. He was returning to his country at the end of the school year."

"It sounds like you may not have received his full attention. That's a shame since it's important to have an excellent advisor your first year to set the right journalistic standards and ethics."

"No, sir, I was lucky I had Ari, er, Mr. Rahani. Yeah, he didn't have as much time as some of the other advisors, but that worked to my benefit. He taught me some shortcuts that I wouldn't have learned otherwise. All my friends at school, particularly the girls, were envious of me."

"Why was that?"

"Well, besides being drop-dead gorgeous and single, he knew how to anticipate and read a situation so he could almost write the story before events unfolded completely. He also has a way of ingratiating himself with movers and shakers in politics."

"How so?"

"By placing information in the media when asked. He taught me the importance of positioning yourself with sources by writing your pieces in a way that helps readers believe the source's perspective is the correct one. Even though he'd been in the country for only a short time, his Rolodex was awesome. He knew all the players in local and state governments. He'd tell all of us in class, and me since he was my advisor, 'Getting the story first counts, nothing else. See the facts you have and anticipate the story from those facts to position the event correctly in the reader's mind.'"

"Oh, my. How interesting. Did he leave the school once he finished that year?"

"Yes, he went back to India."

"Good. Who was your next advisor?"

"Oh, my God, a Ms. Sanderson, an older woman, and you didn't dare call her Julie. That's for sure."

"You obviously didn't get along very well."

"Oh, we got along okay; however, she was a stickler for procedures, not seeing the facts or anticipating and developing sources. The excitement of journalism was less, but it was still there. The boredom of asking the same question to many people who comprise a story became the norm."

Crumby raised both hands and said, "But isn't that what journalism is all about, making sure the facts are correct?"

"Yeah, it was all right, but different from Ari's, er, Mr. Rahani's approach. I'm lucky I had that first year with him to balance my educational experience."

"How so?"

"I got my first internship between my sophomore and junior years, on a paper in a small town near here. That way I could live at home that summer and save money. My beat was politics, and there was a local election coming up in August. In the coverage's course, I came across an obscure bit of information about the current mayor, who was running for reelection."

"What obscure information?"

"Well, there was this local street person, the type in the past you would call the town drunk. He hung around the court-house square. I befriended him, and he became my source."

"How did he become your friend?"

"Everybody knew him because he had been a big high school football star. He couldn't do anything right after high school. He didn't get into college, couldn't hold a job for long because of his drinking. He became one of those objects the town's people didn't see, even when they looked directly at him. Anyway, one day he was hanging, you know, hanging out in front of the diner on the courthouse square. I could tell he was hungry, but no one would even look at him as they entered and exited the restaurant. He didn't beg; he just looked hungry. I was going in for lunch, and I motioned for him to follow me. Inside, I pointed for him to sit in the same booth with me. That was a mistake because he stank to high heaven. We just ate and made small talk, you know, about the weather and the upcoming football season. I told him what I was doing, and he told me his story, nothing about politics.

"After that, when I'd see him around the courthouse, I'd slip him the price of lunch at the diner. It wasn't much, but enough for him to get a meal. He would give me tidbits, mostly gossip and worthless stuff. Then one day he mentioned the mayor was not the good, upstanding citizen he held himself up to be. When I asked what he meant, he just grinned and said I needed to look carefully. That's all he said. I asked around and found out the mayor had kept him from getting a job with the city. I tucked the comment away in my mind. A week later, I was in the courthouse and going from the courtroom side to the side where the mayor and council meet. Passing a door that stood ajar, and that I later realized was a janitorial supply room, I heard this familiar voice talking to someone on the phone. The voice became animated and elevated as the conversation went on. I heard the voice say they could meet at ten-thirty that night. It was a Wednesday night, so I knew most people would be at church for supper and fellowship until nine. I went back to the hallway corner and waited to see who came out of the room. It was the mayor. I did what Ari had taught me. Look at the facts and anticipate. I followed the mayor that night as he took his family home from church and waited to see if he would go back out. He did and went to a rural road and turned onto a gated dirt road into the woods. You know what I mean: a place that looks like a pine tree plantation. I marked the location with my GPS. The next morning, I went back to the location and took pictures of the gate and the road. I then went to the courthouse and looked at the tax records and found the property is owned by an Atlanta LLC."

Crumby uncrossed his legs, sat forward in his seat, smiled, and said, "Did you check the LLC at the state website to see who owned it?"

"No time. I convinced my editor to run a story asking: Why is a family man going to a meeting at 10:30 p.m. to a site owned by an Atlanta corporation?"

Crumby sat back in his seat, a disappointed look on his face. "Go on."

"To make a long story short, the Atlanta media picked the piece up. It turned out the land is owned by a developer who wanted to bring a big-box retailer to a new strip shopping center in our county, which would impact several of the local businesses in the community."

"So, you really didn't get the story?"

"Well, I had the facts and anticipated the correct outcome," Adrienne said defensively. "Yeah, I wish I had learned the name of the developer, but I broke the story of the meeting. The council vote split, and the mayor had the deciding vote. The exposé blew the mayor's race up. From that point on, the shoo-in for the mayor's reelection turned into a landslide for his opponent."

"Interesting. You did good up to a point. You should have taken the time to get the entire story."

"Not enough time. The vote was to be the next week. It was like Ari said: see the facts, anticipate, and break the story first."

"What other highlights did you have in journalism school?"

"That was it. It set me up as a sort of celebrity at school. Most of the professors were complimentary, but some, including Ms. Sanderson, were critical. They assigned me to a different advisor that year."

"Who were you assigned to?"

"A really cool guy, Mr. Epperson. He was working on his PhD."

"Alphonse Epperson—I know him well. He didn't stay very long, if I remember correctly."

"No, he didn't. Mr. Epperson helped instill self-confidence in me. He taught me that politicians were just as human as the rest of us and, most times, had their own agenda that worked against the well-being of the people. He taught me it was my duty as a journalist to expose those politicians who were not for diversity, fairness, and decency."

"Excuse me for interrupting, Adrienne. What definition and measurement of diversity, fairness, and decency did Mr. Epperson use?" Crumby said, shifting forward and looking at Adrienne.

"He said the politicians who wanted lower taxes, smaller government, more military, and spouted about God, country, guns, and patriotism were actually the enemies of ordinary citizens."

"How did he explain that concept?"

"He showed us globalism and diversity fostered world peace. Globalism is good for everyone but better for the poor areas of the world, because it shifts resources from rich countries like ours and Europe and infuses them into underdeveloped nations. Conservatives and nationalists, to use his terms, were against globalization so they could continue to be rich. He said that as journalists, we had an obligation to 'put a nail in the coffin of nationalism' no matter how we had to do it."

"Fascinating. Tell me again, what did he teach you was your job as a journalist?"

"He said people needed us to see the self-interest of conservatives, the importance of tilting in favor of the poor people of the world, and support those who truly want to help others rise in wealth. You know, like, have more opportunities." Adrienne looked at Crumby, searching for some understanding.

"What did he mean by tilting? Can you give me an example?"

Oh God, maybe I've said too much, Adrienne mused as she took a sip of her tea. "Of course," she said. "He used the last senatorial election in Mississippi as a class project. The incumbent senator, I've forgotten his name, was against the Free & Fair-Trade Proposal, called FFTP, and his opponent was for it. First, he had us look up what contributions were being received by the two campaigns and where the funds were coming from."

"That was outstanding work. Go on."

"Once we established that most of the contributions to the opponent were coming from sources favorable to the FFTP, Mr. Epperson had us write articles about the campaign that were tilted to help voters see the benefit of FFTP and the opponent."

"Again, what do you mean by tilting?"

"Like writing an article that implied the incumbent did something negative to his constituents by opposing FFTP, even if that wasn't exactly correct."

"Explain that to me, please," Crumby pressed.

"Suppose the incumbent voted for a budget. We'd comb through the budget and find an expenditure that was not in the constituents' best interest and highlight that fact in an article. In other cases, we took some of the literature handed out by FFTP supporters and adjusted it to look favorable to the citizens of Mississippi, even if there wasn't any direct benefit now and their senator was working against the citizens receiving these benefits. We implied in some pieces that the incumbent was taking campaign contributions from people who were seeking special favors from him."

"Did Mr. Epperson question the ethics of what you were doing? All major campaign contributors are seeking access to the politician, so how is that tilting?"

Adrienne crossed her arms across her chest, trying to clarify her comments. "Like, in this case, we sort of implied that there was a definite connection, assuming there would be one if the incumbent stayed in office. Mr. Epperson taught us how to enhance the power of our journalistic profession."

"Oh, my. How did you feel about this manipulation of your ethics?"

"It wasn't manipulation of our ethics. It was, as he said, 'the power of journalism in its purest form.'"

"Adrienne," Crumby said, sitting ramrod straight, "that's drivel. A journalist's ethics are—no, must be—the bedrock of their existence. Tilting, as you call it, the facts to influence a position isn't journalism; it is propaganda in its vilest form. Real, tough journalists, like Ida Tarbell, who went after John D. Rockefeller, didn't have to manipulate facts, just uncover them and show the dishonesty and collusion. A journalist's job is not to 'win over' readers, but to inform readers so the reader can develop an intelligent opinion about an issue, not re-characterize the issue in favor of one side or the other." Crumby sat forward on the edge of his chair, drumming his finger on the table repeatedly. "Brutal honesty, right down the middle of the road, scooping up all the facts and presenting them in clear language that even a first-grader can understand is what journalism is. Journalists are the watchdogs of a free and open society, not the lapdogs of one side or the other. Those puppeteers, the politicians and their minions who leak privileged information as an opioid, enslaving the journalists who find it easier to be a lapdog than a watchdog, are the real enemies of the people, whether they are conservative, liberal, or progressive. Do you know why?"

"Er, I guess not," Adrienne whispered, shocked by the venomous excitement in Crumby's voice and the redness of his face, even though he hadn't raised his voice or changed his demeanor.

Still pounding the table with his finger hard enough to rattle the teacups on their saucers and the utensils on their plates, he continued, "Because those slimeballs, by hooking the journalists on their stolen information, deprive the people of true, fair, and actionable information, information that may change the outcome of an election or the vote on legislation. Journalists, or I should say, some elitist opinion writers, are lower in regard than used car salespeople and the politicians themselves because they don't go after the facts independently, verify the facts, and show their readers the pros and cons." Crumby slumped back in his chair, shaken by his tirade. He tried to reach for his teacup but had to put his hand on the table to stop it from shaking. "I'm sorry, my dear, for my outburst. As you can see, journalistic ethics and excellence are important to me. I knew Mr. Epperson had moved on, but I did not know how much damage he had done to the three years of students he taught. Sad and shocking," he said, shaking his head. "Now, who was your advisor after they exposed you to Mr. Epperson?"

"Then I got Mrs. Wright my senior year."

"I know Pearl. Was there anything else special about school?"

"No. Between my junior and senior years, I did an internship up in the mountains, where I had the sports and political beats, but nothing much happened. It was so boring."

Crumby interrupted again. "Excuse me for interrupting again, but did you use some of the journalistic principles they taught in school to take the news pulse of the community?"

"Er, not really." Adrienne looked nervously and shifted her gaze to the ocean. "I just tried to keep my eyes and ears open, just as Ari showed me. My senior year, Mrs. Wright had me apply to papers in ten different state capitals. I didn't get an interview at eight but did at two. I was lucky that Mrs. Wright knew the editor-in-chief at those two and got me the interviews. She coached me on some of the key answers to their regular questions; otherwise, I wouldn't have done as well as I did. Some of those questions made it clear to me they were out of the nineteenth century."

Crumby's interest perked up. He uncrossed his legs and shifted in his seat, sitting directly frontal and leaning forward, still focused on Adrienne's eyes. "Please give me an example of what you mean, Adrienne."

Adrienne looked at her teacup. "I'm not sure I remember. Hmm—oh, yeah, one was that they would ask me what my favorite subjects in journalism school were. I told them about investigative techniques and ethics."

"Were they?"

"They were okay, but not really." Adrienne shifted in her seat and looked animated for the second time as her voice and hands seemed to take on another spirit. "The most amazing time was in communications and journalism history. I loved reading about the newspapers in the nineteenth century and their powerful owners, who could sway the public with their fiery stories, whether the stories were truthful or not. Other times, they befriended the business titans of the time, so the papers wouldn't disclose some of their business practices. Just think, they were mostly responsible for the Spanish-American War through their reporting and the slanting of the issues to show their perspective." She looked at Crumby, seeking a reaction, and said, "Sort of like what Mr. Rahani and Mr. Epperson taught us in school." She held her breath.

Crumby swiveled in his seat, crossing his legs, putting both hands in his lap, and continuing to look intently at Adrienne. "Was it right for them to do that?"

Adrienne looked toward the ocean and then focused on the lawn and the lounge chairs filled with sunbathers of all ages and sizes. "I don't know if it was right. Journalism and the people's desire to know what is going on gave them the power to do it, and they seized that power and used it to their advantage and the country's advantage. They had the power and used it. I guess that was their right. Yeah, they had the right to do it, and they did it."

"They had the right, but was it right?"

Adrienne continued looking away from Crumby's stare, shifting her gaze over his shoulder to a good-looking guy in a wildlife officer uniform of a tan shirt, deep-green pants, and brown boots. His shirt had several patches and badges. A falcon sat on a thick leather glove covering his hand and forearm. He was walking around among the lunch crowd. "What's he doing?" she asked, trying to avoid the question.

Crumby turned in his seat and saw the falconer. "*Quiscalus major*, better known as boat-tailed grackles, plague the outside dining here at the Beach Club. These black birds have no fear of taking the food off your plate. They are afraid of falcons, who think grackles are the most delicious meal in the world. So during the season, management hires the falconers from a wildlife plantation to bring a bird up each day and keep the grackles at bay. Seems inefficient, but it works, and the tourists and children think it's neat. You didn't answer my question."

Adrienne was twisting her napkin on her lap. She knew how she answered this question was going to be the key to getting his help. She could feel it. Should she tell him what he wanted to hear, or should she tell him how she felt and remain true to herself? Adrienne took a deep breath, looked into Crumby's eyes, and said, "If you have the power to influence people, you have a responsibility to use it, but you need to know when to use the power, when not to, and for what purpose."

Crumby smiled and nodded his head affirmatively. "Okay, where did you go to work, and why aren't you still there?"

"I went to work for a small paper outside the Atlanta beltway, the *Sentinel Press*. The money was less than the position offered in Little Rock, Arkansas, but the *Sentinel* gave me the local and state political beat, allowing me to not only cover the local politicians but also follow them to the state capitol as they moved up in their careers. The county has several mid-sized and large industrial employers, which gave the local and state representatives, even the district congressman, unusual clout around the capitol. I got lucky, the sports reporter had been at the paper his entire career, and he took me under his wing and showed me the lay of the political land, so to speak."

"The sports reporter? What was his name?"

"High school football in the county rivals the Atlanta Falcons in terms of fan hysteria. All the local and state politicians from Sherman County show up at all the high school games. It's a major constituent glad-handing time. His name is Jason Brubaker. Do you know him?"

"I don't know him, but I know of him. Go on."

"Well, Jason certainly shortened my learning curve, helping me understand the history of all the political players in our county. He helped me separate the liberal politicians from the conservative, nationalist politicians. He sure knew all the shortcuts. Anyway, I guess you want to know what happened."

"No, I know what happened. What I want to know is your side of the affair." Crumby looked at his watch and smiled at Adrienne.

Adrienne looked away and was quiet. For the second time, she felt her eyes burn and tears forming. She willed herself not to cry. Getting through the next few minutes was crucial. *He's got to help me.* She thought of her boyfriend, the beach, and countless other thoughts so she wouldn't cry. Blinking rapidly, she looked back at Crumby and smiled.

Crumby detected a different expression and demeanor, changing her from a young, impassioned, confident journalist cocooned by her psychological defenses, into an insecure adult-child, crushed by the realization that her friends and parents were wrong: she was not a special genius who could conquer her chosen field without hard work, just by working smart. "It's only right that I hear your side of the story," Crumby said, smiling.

"Jason took me under his wing and helped me understand the 'players,' his name for the politicians in our community. He helped me build a dossier on everyone active in county politics. I cross-referenced info between them all. It's amazing to see how every little piece of information, gathered over time, can develop into a clear picture of relationships and common interests."

"Give me an example."

"You know, Councilman A votes for a particular rezoning, saying he or she is interested in bringing jobs to the county. Six months later Councilman B, who had voted against the rezoning since it's in his district and his constituents didn't want it, turns out to be the receiver of a major campaign contribution from the company benefiting from the vote of Councilman A. The rezoning passed, by the way. Councilman B leads the effort to get Councilman A appointed to the State Regents Board, an appointment Councilman A wanted for years. Did I mention that these two councilmen were in different political parties and were supposedly rivals for the mayor's job?"

"Now, that's an excellent journalistic endeavor. Well done," Crumby said with admiration.

"Yeah, anyway, one piece of information Jason gave me was about our congressman. Trey Trawick is an archconservative, very vocal about his Christian religion, and has a reputation for being a womanizer. As Jason said, the congressman is addicted to strange."

"Oh, my, how crude." Crumby sat back quickly, as if someone had slapped him in the face.

"I'm sorry, but that's how he put it, not me. Anyway, the congressman is good friends with Howard Boulder, our state representative, who is best friends with Irwin Friedman, a restaurant and bar owner in Atlanta. Trawick frequented one of these bars, the Git and Split, which was on the southeast side of Atlanta. It's in a mixed neighborhood that's mostly Black, but gentrifying as young professionals working downtown look for a place to live in the urban center. The Git and Split is way outside Trawick's district.

"Well, there was a brouhaha going on in our district about—what else—a rezoning, which was highly divisive. The county commission chair, a guy named Elgin, Wesley "Fats" Elgin, a dedicated liberal democrat, was running against the congressman and was for the rezoning. Trawick, trying to appear neutral, was working behinds the scenes to block the rezoning. The rezoning would turn what had always been a stable lower-class neighborhood of working families into a commercial area, clearly hurting the quiet, residential character of that part of the county. Trawick, even though he's a bible-thumping, staunch NRA supporter, always sided with working people when he felt they were being steamrolled by developers and their politician friends. Jason came to me, saying one of his impeccable sources said Trawick was in town and interested in a young, twenty-something Black server at the Git and Split. Did I mention Trawick is White, in his forties, very rich, from one of the original families that settled that part of the state? Oh, and I almost forgot, he has a wife and four children.

"I decided to see for myself. I grabbed my camera and went over to the bar. It's on the northwest corner of 123rd street and MLK Boulevard. I parked mid-block, across the street from the bar's entry. Once my car was in place, I went into the bar and bought a ginger ale to go. While inside, I saw Trawick in a booth, talking to two Black guys I didn't know. A young woman, probably twenty to twenty-one years old, was serving the table. After I got my ginger ale, I went back to my car, checked my camera, flipped on the date and time function, put on a 75 mm to 200 mm zoom lens, and waited. At 6:00 p.m., Trawick and the young female server came out together. He had his hand on her elbow and they were laughing and talking with each other. It was obvious they knew each other well. I got all of this with my camera. The couple got into his car. I followed them, which was easy because they only drove five or six blocks. They went into a new-looking apartment building, which stood out because everything else on the block was old, derelict, or under renovation. I got more shots of them entering the building. When they went inside, I waited a few minutes and went up to the door where the mailboxes were located. Amanda Kawami, the only young-sounding name, was on a box 2C. I went back to my car, noted the time, and waited until Trawick came out at eight thirty, documenting his departure with more pictures. I left and went back to the newsroom since I had other stories to finish before the 12:15 a.m. press deadline."

"Who was the night editor?" Crumby asked.

"Sid Hernandez."

Crumby shook his head in recognition. "Go on."

"At 11:00 p.m., Josh, er, Jonathan Webster, the crime reporter, and I were talking when we heard a call on the police radio for a possible sexual assault at the address where Trawick and the young Black girl went. He was going over there, and I asked if I could go with him. He said sure because he was always trying to get time with me. We arrived, he talked with one cop he knew, and he found out it was the tenant in 2C, Amanda Kawami. We confirmed she was the server from the Git and Split. The neighbors in 2D said they saw her come in with a White guy and had seen no one else come or go. I knew it was Trawick. By this time, it was 11:45 p.m. We had just thirty minutes to file our story, the biggest story in the state, before the TV and radio media had the story. Besides his heated reelection campaign, Trawick was being talked about for a future statewide race, either for governor or senator. I had my camera and laptop in the car, so I went back to the car and figured I had the scoop of a lifetime."

Adrienne was sitting rigidly in her chair, tears streaming down her cheeks in muddy mascara rivulets, her chest heaving and her hands washing themselves continually in some frantic attempt to cleanse herself. "I didn't accuse Trawick of anything. The article showed he had a relationship with the girl and had the picture of him leaving the bar with her, then leaving her apartment, and then the girl being taken out of the apartment on a stretcher. I added pictures of the police cars and an ambulance. I emailed the story and photos back to the paper.

"Sid called and asked if I had contacted Trawick for comments. If I couldn't get him, the story wouldn't run. He said he'd hold the presses for ten minutes, but no longer. If I couldn't reach Trawick, the story would run the next day. I called his cell number, which is public knowledge, and got a recording. I really wanted the story. Facts appeared clear, and I anticipated what they meant. Besides, he was a politician who professed one image and lived another. I called Sid back and told him Trawick had no comment, and the story ran, front page, above the fold, with the damaging photos."

Crumby took his handkerchief from his sport jacket's left breast pocket and handed it to Adrienne across the table. He had a look of sadness on his face. "We all now know, the young lady was the granddaughter of Trawick's family servant, who had worked for his parents for decades, and she was Trawick's goddaughter, attending Morehouse College. Didn't they arrest two young Black men for the crime the next day? It was something about how they also thought she was dating a White guy and that wasn't right?" Crumby said in a soft tone. "It seems racism is a universal trait, not solely reserved for conservative, bible-thumping, NRA-supporting Whites."

Recovering some composure, Adrienne said, "It's not my fault."

"If it's not your fault, whose fault is it, my dear?"

The Corner Table

NOTE: This story is a work of fiction; however, the description of the High Line and its features is accurate as of the time the story took place. When the High Line first opened it was different than what has evolved as the park and the surrounding neighborhoods gentrified.

"WHY PICK A RESTAURANT near here?" Tom wondered. "I don't understand what is so important she couldn't wait until tonight. With Amy, everything is always important. Now I won't see the new REI store and get one of the freebies." He bounded up the High Line's brushed-steel steps at Thirtieth Street, loosening his tie, unbuttoning his collar and cuffs, and rolling up his sleeves as he climbed. The early June day was warm, not hot, with a steady breeze coming off the Hudson River. Cotton-ball clouds rode the thermals, moving from west to east. As he reached the top step, Tom looked at his watch: twenty minutes to make it to Gansevoort and back to the restaurant—tight but doable. Noticing the chain-link fence that separated the renovated High Line from the old, rusting section of railroad track curving west and north along the Hudson River, circling the railcar collection yard, he recognized the potential for more. Even in its unrepaired condition, the closed railbed to the north gave a glimpse of the future. High Line staff had two shipping containers with double doors cut into the sides, painted in a black-and-white zebra motif. These served as their toolsheds and hangout place close to the Thirtieth Street stairway. Turning to his left, heading south, he looked up, stopped, and smiled. A lone girl sat reading on a long, curved bench. She wore a sleeveless navy tank top and wild navy-and-white-striped pants. Her feet were on the bench, knees together and feet apart. "Isn't she worth knowing?" he mused until he looked past the girl to the building abutting the walkway. The entire five-story stark-white building overlooking the High Line had large black circles in symmetrical rows with a facial portrait of an Asian man in the middle, stretching from the roof to the base of the High Line's side benches. Short black bangs covered the forehead, the eyes squinted almost shut, and the mouth appeared to utter a guttural sound, as if he was delivering a lethal blow. Menacing diagonal streaks of black war paint crossed his face, adding to the aggressiveness. Tom's excitement built as he continued moving south.

"Awesome," he said aloud, more to himself than anyone else, as he surveyed the transformed, elevated railway weaving its path between former warehouses, industrial buildings, and low-rent apartments on the city's west side, from Thirtieth Street in Chelsea to Gansevoort Street in the Meatpacking District. Tom reached into his pocket, took out his iPhone, and began snapping photographs and shooting video for his friends at O'Reilly's High & Not Dry Saloon later. He moved along the concrete walkway, past the benches containing people eating lunch, reading, talking, or sitting with their eyes closed. White buds protruded from ears as they enjoyed a world of their own making. Lining both sides of the raised railbed-turned-walkway between Thirtieth and Twenty-Sixth streets, benches flanked by dense Mexican feather grass, daises, sunflowers, and dogwood and sumac trees, were one venue for watching the parade of humanity, taking in the unique perspective both above and within the beating heart of the city. Looking right and left as he moved, snapping photos of the industrial buildings, street commerce, and river vistas, he delighted in the graffiti, which was obviously created for the High Line trekkers. Some buildings, mostly the old, dirty, brown brick ones, sported single cartoon caricatures painted in hard-to-reach places, their existence a testament to the fearlessness and skills of the artists. Whole sides of buildings, as well as rooftops of one- and two-story buildings lower in elevation than the High Line, were now art installations simply because the High Line existed.

At Twenty-Sixth Street, Tom saw the walkway move up, forming a flyover separate from the old railbed. Trees, shrubs, and plants were now below the walkway, giving visitors a unique perspective of the lush vegetation. At Twenty-Fifth, the walkway sloped down, reuniting with the main railbed as it passed between tall buildings, causing the sensation of moving through a narrow gorge. He thought that two-level expanse was cool and wondered if the lower level was open. Tom noticed the lock on the gate. No going in there. That's a shame; it would be an interesting place to take a girl. Looking up from his investigation of the lower-level thicket, Tom viewed wooden bleachers and a stretch of lawn, a sunny place to come and just hang out. He knew babes in bikinis would be on this lawn and bleachers this weekend.

Checking his watch, he approached the bird and butterfly boxes and feeding trays fanning out and up on both sides of the walkway, secured to taut wire, between Twenty-First and Twenty-Second streets. Tom stepped backward toward the grasses and foliage, shooting some iPhone video. He tripped over the raised lip of the molded concrete walkway. Stones were embedded in the smooth fabricated walkway, which had long slits for growing the thick grasses hanging over the path. Tom shot video of tourists craning their necks to see in the minute box openings, holding their cameras ready to capture any birds or butterflies unlucky enough to be in residence. Slices of apples and pears stood erect in clips, luring migratory flyers to rest and refresh. Tom quickened his pace. He wanted to make it all the way to Gansevoort Street before meeting Amy at La Lunchonette on the corner of Eighteenth Street and Tenth Avenue. None of his friends had been to the High Line, and he wanted to be the first, with pictures and videos to prove it.

At Eighteenth street, Tom looked east and saw an old, tan-and-brown four-story building with La Lunchonette 1988 painted on the side. Why there? Obviously, no chic retail shops in there. Seven blocks to the end and seven back, with ten minutes to go. No problem. He kept moving.

Between Sixteenth and Fifteenth streets, he let out a low whistle and grinned as he looked at the tiered amphitheater with a wall of glass hanging below the High Line, above the middle of Tenth Avenue, with traffic moving north at a rapid pace. The wooden benches and pathways leading to the bottom were full of people, mostly young, eating their lunch and talking. He noticed a mother pushing a baby stroller down the sloping aisle, searching for a place to sit, balancing a cup and paper bag in one hand. Tom looked around and caught the eye of a twenty-something having lunch with her girlfriend, both with their skirts hiked up as far as they could, their thighs tightly closed, and their shirts unbuttoned enough to hang off their shoulders. She smiled and, he perceived, ever so slightly shifted her legs in a way Tom took as an invitation. He couldn't believe the scene on this elevated world of interest. The High Line changed character at this spot. Space for trees, thicker foliage, and more people fanned out as the elevated park prepared to enter a building. The ribbon-like spaces between Thirtieth Street and Sixteenth Street gave way to spaces with tables and chairs and corners screened off by foliage, inviting private conversations.

At the amphitheater, the park curved to the east and entered the Chelsea Market building just as the original railbed entered this and other industrial buildings and warehouses, formerly delivering goods to now-vanished manufacturers and processors. The walkway took two routes through this covered space. The wider east path held vendors selling souvenirs, art, and food in a space large enough for group activities, including receptions, plays, dances, and exercise classes. The lower westside walkway was an outdoor café with patrons eating, resting, and people-watching. He scanned the menu for another time when he would bring Amy on her first visit to the High Line. Moving up the steps to the higher eastern path, Tom retrieved his iPhone from his shirt pocket and shot video of visitors of all ages, shoeless and splashing in a section of the walkway, wet from a constant stream of water deep enough to delight a child or child-at-heart. He looked around and saw singles and couples reclining on wooden chaise lounges lined up to face the Hudson River to the west. Checking his watch and picking up his pace, Tom noticed this southern end of the High Line contained dense stands of dogwood, sumac, and holly trees. Gone were the Mexican grasses and annual or perennial flowers. At Gansevoort Street, Tom acknowledged a billboard declaring the future site of the Whitney Museum, one of his favorite museums. He turned, heading back to the Eighteenth Street stairs.

Taking the exit stairs two at a time, Tom saw a taxi turn right onto Tenth avenue from Seventeenth street and roll to a stop at the corner of Eighteenth, in front of the brown and tan building he saw earlier. A medium-height, slender woman in her late twenties with shoulder-length auburn hair emerged from the taxi's curbside rear door. She wore a light-gray, tailored suit with a white scoop-necked blouse and a string of black pearls with matching earrings. A black Ricky bag was hooked over her shoulder. Looking around, she stood elegantly erect, like a royal princess surveying her domain. Her calves, accentuated by her four-inch-high black Ferragamo pumps, exhibited the muscular form of a runner. Amy saw Tom crossing Tenth Avenue and assumed the slight smile she wore when first meeting a client in her work, friendly but all business. She breathed deeply to calm herself.

"Hi, Amy!" Tom called out as he waved to get her attention. Reaching her, they embraced lightly, and Tom kissed her on the cheek.

"I'm sorry I'm late. The doctor was running behind," she said.

"It's cool. I thought I was going to be late. I walked the entire length of the High Line, and I can't wait to show it to you. It's awesome," Tom enthused as he steered Amy, his hand on the small of her back, toward the side door of the restaurant.

Heading for the graffiti-scarred door, Tom stared at a statue of the Virgin Mary in the window along with a sun-faded and cracked menu, both protected behind a thick single pane of chicken-wire-embedded glass. When lowered, a metal roll-down shutter encased in its overhead compartment, painted a dark brown to match the lower half of the building, protected the carved eight-panel wooden door from the graffiti artists. The left channel of the shutter blazed with graffiti. Tom wondered if the roll-down itself had stylized graffiti or if it was a free-flowing design. He opened the door for Amy and followed her in. The cool darkness of the interior enveloped them.

A smiling woman with bleached blond hair, older than Amy, in a white tank top and black jeans, with elaborate tattoos on both arms and shoulders, approached from behind the cluttered bar. "Bonjour. Deux?"

"Bonjour," Amy responded and nodded.

"S'il vous plait, me suivre," the hostess said as she steered them toward the front barroom on their left. The room was half full and noisy.

"Le pardon; avez-vous une table dans um tout à fait coin?" Amy asked.

"Oui, cette façon," the hostess responded, smiling, turning, and leading them to a table for two near a window in the back dining room.

"Est-ceci satisfaisant?" She asked, holding out the chair for Amy.

"Parfait," Amy responded, taking the seat while putting her handbag on the floor, leaning against the wall.

"My name is Miriam, and I'll be your server today. May I bring you tap, flat, or sparkling water?"

"Tap water," Tom responded, "and two glasses of Chablis."

"No wine for me," Amy interjected. "I'll have tea, please."

"Hot or iced?" Miriam asked, turning to look at Amy.

"Iced, please."

"Sugar or sweeteners?"

"None, thank you."

Walking over to the wall, Miriam picked up a blackboard, a chalk menu in a mixture of French and English. Returning to Tom and Amy's table, she placed the menu on the floor, leaning it against the back of a chair at the next table.

"I'll be right back with your drinks."

Tom placed his phone on the table.

"Please turn that off and put it up," Amy asked. "Can't we have a pleasant lunch with conversation instead of tweets, texts, or emails?"

"Okay," Tom said, turning off the phone and putting it in his shirt pocket.

Tom and Amy turned their attention to the menu and Tom asked, "How come no wine with lunch?"

"I don't want any. Um, I've—got a busy schedule this afternoon," Amy stammered.

The hostess returned with their drinks, a small basket of bread, and a plate of butter. "Any questions?"

"I'll have the ham omelet, please," Amy said, smiling at Miriam.

"I'll have the goat cheese puff pastry." Tom said, reaching for a slice of baguette and his knife.

"Excellent choices," Miriam said, turning from the table.

"Why this place?" Tom asked.

"It reminds me of the café we ran into when we got caught in the rain in Paris, the day we went to the Museé du Luxenbourg," Amy said. "You know, the one on Bis Servandoni between Rue Férou and Rue Garanciére, in the sixth arrondissement."

"If you say so," Tom said, looking around. La Lunchonette was typical of the many neighborhood cafes they enjoyed in Paris five weeks ago: dark walls with a lot of wood, a slight down-on-our-luck look, utilitarian tables with white butcher paper over a white tablecloth, and plain, dark wood and brown leather-backed chairs, worn with use, probably the same ones placed in the restaurant when it opened in 1988. Pepper mills and glass sugar jars served as centerpieces. Cheap, stamped-metal knives and forks on white napkins and upside-down glasses waited for patrons. Window light was the predominant daytime illumination. A few photographs, framed prints, wine advertisements, and a large horizontal mirror in a gilded frame, most of them canted to either side from time and gravity, were the wall decorations. A red Coca-Cola clock on the back wall seemed totally out of place, its face tilted to the right. The masculine, polished wood bar held excess glasses, serving pitchers, extra sugar jars, and a tray of tableware. Obviously, there was no sitting or standing at the bar. Tom thought that was a shame.

Looking back at Amy, Tom said, "I see what you mean. How did you find it?"

"I came here a week ago with a group from the office. Remember, I told you I'm serving as senior advisor-associate on a team headed by that new associate, Reggie Boykin? Well, as team leader, he thought it would be good for all of us to get together away from the office to discuss our strategy for obtaining the Oatley & Co. engagement."

"Oh, yeah, the distinguished Reginald Andrew Boykin the Fourth. Why aren't you team leader? You're the senior associate at the firm and possibly the partner-to-be in a few months," Tom said, buttering another slice of bread.

"Do you ever listen to me? A year ago, I told you about this guy, Reggie. He's older than any other associate. Between his junior and senior years of college, he dropped out and sold all his possessions except for his bicycle and a set of *The Great Books* he bought for $150. He moved to Ballard Ridge, Virginia, rented a furnished one-room garage apartment, and did yard work to get by. He says he got up every day at 6:00 a.m., read for four hours, did yard work for four hours, and then either walked around town or rode his bike out to a trailhead for hiking. Eighteen months later he finished reading the books, re-enrolled for his senior year, graduated, and entered NYU's law and MBA joint degree program. He graduated with honors."

"Why yard work?" Tom asked, reaching for another slice of bread. "That's kind of nothing, not like guiding fishing, kayaking, or hunting trips."

"He said his purpose was to read and reflect on what he read and how fragile life is. Yard work is physical, not mental. As he worked, he thought about what he read. When some special idea came to him, he'd jot it down on a pad he always carries with him."

"Hmm. What great life secret did he learn during this chill-out time?" Tom asked, tipping his wineglass to his lips.

"I asked him that, too. He says he doesn't want to ever take life for granted."

"Anyway, why come back to a place that reminds you of a rain-drenched Paris afternoon?" Tom said, sitting back in his chair, smiling at Amy.

Amy, about to answer, saw the hostess approaching with their lunches. Miriam placed their plates in front of them. Amy looked at her omelet and realized it would feed both of them. Tom grinned as Miriam placed his goat cheese pastry on salad greens in front of him.

"May I bring you anything else?" Miriam asked.

"How about more bread?" Tom asked, holding up and wiggling the empty breadbasket.

"Certainly," Miriam said, taking the basket and turning away.

"This goat cheese is enough for both of us," Tom said, picking up his knife and fork. "Will you eat some?"

"No, but I'm giving you part of my omelet," Amy responded, cutting her ham and egg lunch in two, slipping her knife under the larger piece, balancing it with her fork on top, and passing it over to Tom's plate.

Making room on his plate for the offered omelet, Tom replied, "Sure, I'll take half, but you need to take some of my goat cheese." Tom took a bite and a sip of wine. "Oh my God, this is amazing. Are you sure you don't want some?"

Miriam returned, placing another basket of bread on the table. "Merci," Amy said, smiling at her. Turning her attention back to Tom, Amy said, "No, thank you."

"Okay, why does this place remind you of that Paris café? There are better cafes we enjoyed while over there."

"The bathroom," Amy said, blushing and smiling.

"The bathroom? I don't understand."

"You don't remember? We were dripping wet, went into the loo to dry off, and when I unbuttoned my blouse to take off my bra, you started drying my breast. You don't remember the corner table we thought was going to collapse?"

"Oh, yeah. Your concern was the rickety table, but I focused on more pleasant aspects. Getting a quickie with a café full of Frenches eating lunch outside the door was great," Tom said, grinning with satisfaction and saluting Amy with his wineglass.

Amy leaned forward, looking directly into Tom's eyes. "It wasn't just a quickie for me. It was different, special. When you came inside me, I felt a sensation wash over my insides. Not an orgasm, something I can't explain. I've never felt a change like that before or since. The physical and emotional sensations were special. I don't know why, they just were. That's all I can say."

Tom leaned back in his chair, still grinning. "We always have good sex."

"It wasn't just sex," Amy retorted, sitting back in her chair, shaking her head from side to side. "Do you ever feel sex is as much emotional as physical?"

"Now I understand. I guess so—I don't know what you mean," Tom said, sitting up and taking another bite of his pastry and a sip of wine. "Sure you don't want some goat cheese? It's good."

"No, thank you," Amy said, picking at her omelet and looking across the room, lost in thought.

"Is it because of what I said last night?"

"What?"

"Is it because of what I said last night?"

"What did you say last night?"

"You know, when I teased you about getting a pooch."

"No," Amy said, rolling her eyes and looking away.

"I didn't mean it," Tom said.

Amy turned to look at Tom again. "That's interesting, because you said it, didn't you?" Amy put down her fork and pushed away her plate. "How's your new job going?"

"It's fine. The training is over. I'm assigned to the dividend department."

"Do you like it?"

"Financial operations suck. It helps pay my share of our rent. It's the same thing day after day. Nothing cool like being a park ranger or guiding people on hunting or fishing trips."

"Tom, what do you want to be doing five or ten years from now? Do you think about that?" Amy leaned forward, looking intensely at Tom.

"Hell, no. I'll be thirty in a couple of months. There's too much living to do instead of worrying about five or ten years from now. I'll be doing something I'm passionate about, making a lot of money doing it. What that'll be, I don't know. I'm interested in life now, not trying to figure out how to be a suit in ten years," Tom said, shifting in his chair and reaching for his near-empty wineglass. His eyes looked at his plate and then the breadbasket.

"What about a family? What if we want to have a baby?" Amy said hesitantly, looking down at her plate and reaching for her iced tea glass.

Tom's head snapped up, and he looked at Amy. "I don't want a baby! Jesus, are you crazy? We have a good life. There's plenty of time for strollers, shitty diapers, and no sleep," Tom barked, shaking his head. "God, don't even talk about babies."

"Excuse me, Tom. I just asked. Babies happen, you know," Amy snapped, her eyes wide from Tom's emphatic rejection of a baby.

"That's why they have abortion clinics," Tom retorted, leaning forward, the two of them staring intently at each other.

"You—you could do that to our—your creation?" Amy said, sitting upright. Her eye rims and face turned crimson and her chin quivered slightly before she caught herself and regained composure.

"Yes, of course," Tom said, glaring at Amy.

"Damn, that's a tough decision," Amy said, looking out the window. For the first time she saw the small, wooden man doll sitting on a miniature chair on the windowsill next to a headless, armless, and legless naked female torso. An oversized clay pot holding a dying begonia sat on the other side of the torso, filling up the space. A strange window combination for a restaurant, Amy thought, as she digested the implications of Tom's vehement response to the hint of a baby.

Tom sat back in his seat and said, "Look, you're set in your career. You make good money. We get by pretty good. Ten years from now, I'll be doing something that makes the money you do. I just don't know what, nor do I care about that right now. We're in the sweet spot of life, so why talk about the unknown future? Babies aren't part of our life. Forget about that. I was thinking, I just walked the High Line. You haven't seen it yet. Let's go on the High Line Saturday morning. We'll take a picnic lunch and hang with people up there. There are so many cool places for two people to be alone or meet others."

"I know," Amy interjected.

"What do you mean, you know? We haven't been there."

"Reggie and I went up to the High Line after the lunch meeting."

"Oh? What did you and Reggie go up there for?" Tom scooted forward in his chair.

"To discuss the strengths and weaknesses of the Oatley team and show me how the High Line is changing Chelsea and the Meatpacking District."

"The graffiti is so cool, and so are the art installations," Tom said after finishing his wine.

"Not just the graffiti and outsider art," Amy responded, "but also the demolition and new construction. The opportunities to finance these projects, as well as joint venturing and syndicating projects, are enormous. He set up a spreadsheet detailing property ownership on each side of the High Line from the Hudson River to Seventh Avenue. He's already contacting owners, soliciting their business, and coming up with ideas to work together."

"Well, do you want to picnic Saturday?"

"I can't in the morning. Reggie has called a team meeting that will last until four. We can go then, bring a light dinner with us, and watch the sun go down," Amy said, smiling.

"That's okay. Maybe another time. I'm hanging with Billy and Scott then. We're kayaking the Hudson."

Miriam seated a man and a woman, both in navy pinstriped suits, at the table next to Amy and Tom. Amy noticed they both carried leather briefcases, his scuffed and worn, hers new and smooth. Miriam turned the menu so the new couple could read it and took their drink orders. She left and returned balancing three cassoulets in her hands for three construction workers in grimy T-shirts, dirty jeans, and dust-covered brogans at a nearby table. The workers' hard hats sat on the floor under each chair. She refilled their water glasses and walked over to Amy and Tom. Picking up their plates, she asked, "Did you save room for dessert?"

"No, thank you," Tom and Amy answered in unison.

"Est-ce que ce sera séparée ou ensamble?" Miriam asked, looking at Amy.

"Séparée," Amy responded, reaching for her Ricky bag and smiling at Tom.

Acknowledgements

A big thank you needs to go to my assistant Sheree Adams for keeping all of the logistical work flowing smoothly between the various parties in this endeavor.

Luke Palder and his team at ProofreadingServices.com did their usual outstanding job of copyediting and proofreading. Any residual mistakes are mine.

Ghislain Viau of Creative Book Design did his excellent work on making sure the cover and interior design appeals to readers.

Judy, my wife, muse, motivator, and best critic kept me on course to finish this project.

www.ingramcontent.com/pod-product-compliance
Lightning Source LLC
Chambersburg PA
CBHW021242200726
48288CB00014B/990